Sonia Zylberberg

The Yarmulka in the Window

The Yarmulka in the Window

ISBN-13: 978-0-9877899-3-8 (Sonia Zylberberg)
BISAC: Fiction / Mystery & detective / General

Cover photographs by Sonia Ribaux.
Cover art by Marilyn Bronstein.
Technical consulting for cover by Mona Wizenberg.

I wish to thank

Sonia Ribaux and
Marilyn Bronstein,
whose enthusiasm and creativity
inspired me to continue;

Louise Houle, Régine Miller, Diana Yaros
and Philip Zylberberg, who read and
suggested;

and my dear friend and editor,
Rose Ftaya,
whose commitment and persistence made
this book possible.

For Diana

Table of Contents

Week 1

He crouched in the darkness, listening for any sound. When he was reasonably sure no one was around, he stood up slowly. Now that the moment was here, he wasn't sure he could go through with it. The fear gripped his heart, constricted his lungs and throat so he couldn't breathe. He'd tried to think of everything but there was so much room for error. He wasn't sure their magic charm was powerful enough. He could still turn back, turn around, go on living the way he had been for the last two years. But the gentle, trusting presence of his brother kept him facing forward, this was the only way he could think of to save him, and to keep him safe. So he quieted his heart and forced the air into his lungs; he fingered the small pouch in his pocket, kissed the two halves of the bird amulet his mother had given him, then noiselessly opened the door he'd carefully and secretly oiled the day before, and, taking his brother by the hand, slipped into the night.

∞

HUMMING TO HERSELF, Bella unlocked the door, turned off the alarm, and stepped into her store. She loved the way that sounded: *my* store. She'd worked at Belles Fleurs forever. In fact, it was the only place she'd ever worked since leaving high school. For the last few years, she'd been pretty well managing it by herself, as Jean-Pierre became more and more occupied with the rest of his life. But somehow, since she'd become part owner last year, she'd come to feel differently towards the little flower shop. This proprietary pride was new to her, a big surprise – she'd never thought she'd want to own anything! And here she was, surveying what she'd come to think of as her kingdom, feeling her heart swell with a cautious happiness.

"Hello, hello, my darlings, time to wake up," she whispered to her plants and flowers. As she opened the blinds, she increased the volume of her song and spun around in the now sun-filled store, welcoming each flower, each bud, each leaf into the day.

Her circle brought her back to the front door and she froze in mid-whirl. She was not alone. The huge grin on the face of the stranger left no doubt that she'd been caught in her welcoming act. She felt her cheeks redden and her arms collapse.

"Oh, yes ... uh ... hello ... um ...," she stammered, failing in her attempt at nonchalance. The grin widened as he said, "That was lovely."

"Oh ... mm ... thank you. Were you looking for anything in particular?" she asked, moving the conversation on, giving her burning cheeks a chance to cool down.

"Oh, yes, of course. Your beautiful dancing made me forget why I was here!" He pulled a small poster from the bag slung over his shoulder. "We are just opening our store, in the next block, and I want to invite you to the grand opening. Also, if you wouldn't mind putting this up somewhere ...?"

She carefully examined the poster he'd handed her, glad for something to hide behind. "*objets* – what kind of store is that?"

"Well," he laughed, "a little of this and a bit of that ... it's hard to describe. Come see for yourself!" He removed his hat and swept down in a gracious bow. "Next Monday, from 5 to 7." As he put his hat back on, the grin reappeared. "I look forward to seeing you again," he said, and left.

Bella sat down, her legs suddenly weak, maybe it was because she wasn't used to so much excitement first thing in the morning, or maybe because she'd been caught in such an uncharacteristically revealing display. *Or maybe, just maybe,* a little voice inside whispered, *because he's hot!* That teasing smile .... Perhaps the racing of her heart was not entirely due to embarrassment!

She sat a moment more, savouring the sensation of attraction, then got up to finish her store-opening routine. After looking around carefully to make sure she really was alone, she resumed her serenade to the plants, but quietly this time, almost under her breath: "You don't mind, do you, my pretty ones? I love you just as much, even at a lower volume."

∞

NOISE, MORE NOISE, so much it hurt his ears, but he couldn't move his hands to cover them. His mother lay on top of him, keeping him immobile, her hand covering his mouth to keep him quiet.

Smoke everywhere, and the smell of fire.

All around them, people screaming and crying and shouting. Gunfire and more gunfire. His mother crying silently while she shielded him with her body.

After a very long time, silence. Sitting up slowly. There, a head lying next to them, open eyes staring. A headless body a few feet away.

He tried to scream, but his mother's hand still covered his mouth. She jerked her head in warning.

∞

A VERY PREGNANT NOEMI staggered in and plunked herself down on the dilapidated settee that served as the visitor's chair. Bella left her watering to come over and sit on the only other chair. "Hi, what's up? Are you feeling worse?" she asked her grumpy-looking visitor.

"What could be worse?" was the cranky reply. "Still over a month to go with this … this … THING in my belly, that just keeps getting bigger and bigger with no consideration at all of my back and feet, not to mention my legs and bladder!"

Her frown vanished. "There! I feel much better now! Nothing like a little whining!"

"Glad to be of service." Bella returned her smile. "Is it really worse?"

"Probably not. But I can't whine to Avi – he freaks out and gets all worried."

"Well, feel free to come whine here. Do you want some tea? Or water? Or anything?"

"No tea – I'm too hot. I should have planned this so I was pregnant in the winter!"

"Then you would have complained about being cold and having to wear such heavy clothes," was the unsympathetic response. "I'll get you some juice."

"Thanks, I really do appreciate it. I'll try to control my bellyaching. Ha, ha."

When Bella returned with juice, Noemi was holding the poster that she'd set on her desk and immediately forgotten. "What's this? A new store? What does that mean: '*objets*'? What kind of objects?"

"I don't know. I asked, but he said I would have to come and see." Bella tried to say this in a normal tone, though she couldn't stop her cheeks from flushing.

Luckily, Noemi was too absorbed in her own thoughts to notice. She sighed as she sipped the juice. "Actually, I have a bigger problem to whine about. Do you have time to listen?"

Bella was surprised, as they were not particularly close. It was only recently that Noemi had taken to coming in several times a week, to rest her tired feet during her doctor-mandated walks, and had started talking to her. Bella didn't mind; she liked her and her husband Avi, Moroccan-via-Israel Jews whose Jewishness was very different from the one she'd grown up with. She especially liked the food they'd introduced her to.

She surveyed the quiet store – it was the mid-afternoon lull on a hot summer's day – and said, "As long as you don't mind me jumping up if someone comes in, Raoul's away this month. What's up?"

"It's because it's a boy," Noemi exploded. "Avi assumes we'll circumcise him but I can't bear the thought!"

"Oh." Bella had no idea how to respond.

Noemi didn't need more: "It's barbaric! It's mutilation! It's a throwback to an ancient time and we should never, *never* do it anymore!"

As Bella had no opinion whatsoever on the subject, she could only repeat her "Oh."

Again satisfied with the minimal reaction, Noemi ranted on. "Avi can't see it. He says we have to do it, that it's fundamental, basic, we HAVE to. It's the covenant with God, whatever that means! That it's what Jews do, and we're Jews and our son will be a Jew. So we'll do it. There's no discussion, no reasoning with him."

"I suppose there's no middle ground?" Bella asked, trying to lighten the atmosphere by invoking the image of a half snip. Noemi talked over her, oblivious: "I just won't do it. I refuse to subject the child of my body, the fruit of my womb, to such an outrageous, gross, violation of his body, his very self! I just won't do it!"

They sat in silence for a moment.

"I'm guessing that didn't go over so well with Avi?" Bella ventured.

"His family is even coming. His parents and sister. From Israel. For the occasion. They're just waiting to know when it will take place to book their tickets," was the gloomy reply.

"Not your family?"

"No. Mine will come later, when it's more convenient for everyone. They're not religious. Unlike Avi's."

"Do you get along with his parents?"

"They're okay, but very traditional. I think Avi's afraid of their reaction if we don't do the circumcision. Some things are easy when we're so far away because he doesn't have to tell them. But this one is hard to fake!" She grimaced at Bella, and added, "Thanks for listening. I don't know what we'll do, but it's hard to talk to him about it, he gets so worked up, and you're one of the only Jews I know here."

"Not a very knowledgeable one, I'm afraid. I don't know much about Jewish customs, I've never been to a circumcision.'

Noemi got to her feet, groaning as they took her full weight. "Well, we'll have some kind of ceremony even if it doesn't include snipping, so I hope you'll come?"

"With his very traditional family?" Bella asked doubtfully.

"Yes!" was the firm response. "We'll need all the non-traditional Jews we can get to balance things out. Especially if there is no cutting."

Bella closed the door behind Noemi with a sigh of relief. *What a thing to have to deal with!* She couldn't imagine making a decision like that for another human being.

Before she could forget again, she took the *objets* poster over to the window. As she taped it up in a corner, she remembered that it was past time to change the display. She examined it with a critical eye. Raoul, her part-time helper, had been designing and arranging the window ever since he'd demonstrated his far superior skill. It was working out well: his outlandish tendencies were toned down at her request and her conservative taste was expanded by seeing how much people liked his work. But Raoul was away and the display had already been in place for more than two weeks. Her dilemma was whether to wait for his return or risk doing it herself. She couldn't decide, so, at least for the time being, Raoul's summer garden remained in place.

Week 2

Peace came, and it lasted long enough for him to fence off his early experiences of gunfire and death. For a while he forgot, until he found himself lying on top of his brother, in the darkest and most inconspicuous corner they could find, his hand firmly clamped around his brother's mouth, shielding the little boy with his own body, the fighting raging all around them. Noise and smoke filled the air. 'Then' and 'now' converged. His body remembered. He remembered. He remembered that they'd survived then and it gave him hope that they would this time too. Bolstered by this faith, he lifted his head cautiously, just in time to see his neighbour torn apart by a sudden blast. He pulled the toddler more tightly towards him and curled them both into an even smaller ball.

∞

BELLES FLEURS WAS CLOSED Sundays and Mondays. Sometimes Bella went in on Mondays to do the admin, such as inventory, ordering, the week's accounts but, if she was lucky, which happened more often during the quiet summer months, sometimes she got everything done during regular store hours and had the luxury of two full days off. This was one of those weeks and she took full advantage of the time, spending it quietly with herself, her books, and her TV, resting up and talking to no one.

It was late Monday afternoon when she dragged herself up from her lethargy, prodded by hunger pangs. Her empty fridge offered no relief and, as she munched on a lonely chunk of cheese, she tried to convince herself to go food shopping. Instead, she phoned her downstairs neighbour, hoping Mathieu would have food she could scrounge. Voicemail quashed that hope. Mathieu, she remembered, was away for a couple of weeks visiting his parents in the country.

Her hunger pangs grew more insistent. She could always order in. Her brain lit up at the thought, but she suppressed the idea: *No! You eat junk too often and you know if you don't go shopping today, you'll do this all week again. Like last week. Which is why your fridge is so empty.* "The voice of reason, who needs it," she grumbled, reaching for her backpack .

Outside, the breeze revived her and her pace picked up. As she strode along, enjoying the sensation of moving after two days of couch-ing, her ears were assailed by sounds of music and laughter. Her squinting eyes took in a blaze of colours and a vaguely familiar sign in the store window. Although generally reluctant to join groups, her curiosity was piqued and she approached.

The elegantly scripted 'objets' jogged her memory: The opening of the new store! Uh, oh. Not fond of parties, Bella was about to continue on her errand, when her nose caught the unmistakable aroma of food and her stomach growled loudly. *That one small piece of cheese was digested long ago*, it whispered, *let's go see what they have. After all, we were invited.*

I guess ... I could just drop in, say hello, see what there is to eat, and then leave ... after all, I was invited ....

She plunged into the group of smokers and drinkers and through the narrow doorway festooned with streamers and balloons. Inside, the sudden absence of sunlight caused her to stand still for a moment to get her bearings. A white grin materialized in front of her and, like the Cheshire Cat's, it appeared to have discarded its body. As her eyes adjusted to the dimness, Bella saw that it was her visitor from the previous week, his black skin blending with the darkness of the room.

"Hello!" he said. "I wasn't sure you would come."

"Yes, well ... here I am," she began awkwardly. She seemed to have no ability to speak normally with this man! As he continued to grin at her, she felt compelled to go on talking. "Lots of people here," she said inanely, looking around. "Do you know all of them?"

"Some," he replied. "My partner knows most of them."

"Oh! Your partner...."

"Yes, Zelda. There she is." He waved and, from across the room, a figure wafted towards them, skirts billowing out around her.

"Zelda, meet our neighbour, from the beautiful flower shop down the street." Turning to Bella, he said, "But I don't even know your name."

"Nor I, yours." In case that had sounded cold, she stuck out her hand, saying, "Bella."

He took her hand and, instead of shaking it, lifted it to his lips. "Daniel. And this is my partner Zelda."

Bella retrieved her hand and extended it to Zelda, who gave it a traditional shake, saying, "Very pleased to meet you. Please help yourself to food and drink," and motioning to the table from where the enticing smells emanated. "Thanks!" Bella smiled in genuine appreciation and, as her hosts turned to greet another arrival, went to appease her growling stomach.

Partner? Oh well, another tasty man already taken. She looks a little old for him ... but lots of men are into older women. She'd thought he was flirting with her, but maybe it was a cultural difference; his slight accent in both English and French suggested that neither one was his mother tongue. No doubt she'd misread him and she was glad to have found out before she totally humiliated herself. *As you already have,* her inner voice reminded her.

She regarded the eclectic array of foods in front of her, wondering if it would be too piggish to take some of everything. *Well, after all,* she reminded herself again, *I was invited. Yes, but so were most of the people here, and they probably hadn't figured on actually providing an entire meal for the guests.* She settled on filling the small plate half full: enough to quiet her innards but not enough to seriously deplete the offerings. Turning regretfully away from the food, she was caught by a whiff of what had lured her in in the first place, which she traced to a platter she'd overlooked. She couldn't resist and, with just a touch of guilt, reached for one of the small succulent looking pastries.

"Excellent choice!" The voice in her ear startled her into almost dropping her plate. The pastry hung precariously in mid-air before being rescued by a hand that swept out from behind her and deposited it safely on the dish. The same voice continued: "Can't have you wasting these!"

Bella turned to the man, not sure if she should thank him for saving or berate him for endangering it in the first place. His laughter guided her to a neutral middle ground: "Did you make them?"

"No, not me. But I eat them!"

"What are they?" Bella was pretty sure she would have remembered such a tantalizing aroma if she'd met it before.

"Pupusas." He laughed again at her blank look. "My mother makes them."

Bella finally bit into the pastry and a cheesy bean mixture flowed into her mouth. "This is delicious! Did your mother make these ones?"

"Yes. They are better warm, but she thought they would be okay for here."

"Well, she's right!" Bella concurred, as she shoved the rest of the pastry into her mouth.

When she had swallowed, she added, "Thank your mother for me."

"I would if I knew your name."

"Oh sorry." She wiped her hand on a napkin and, for the second time that evening, stuck it out to introduce herself. "Bella."

Again, her hand was grasped. But instead of raising it to his lips, this man held onto it as his eyes swept over her.

"Aaah," he murmured appreciatively, "Bella indeed. In fact, I would say, Bellísima."

Bella was glad the dim lighting hid her blushes, she really was not used to these flirty men. Struggling to sound unflustered, she ignored his remark and his roving look, and pointedly asked, "And you are?"

"Yes of course, where are my manners? I am Pedro." He held onto her a moment more, gazing into her eyes intensely, before slowly letting go.

She reclaimed her hand and cleared her throat. "Yes, well, pleased to meet you, Pedro," she responded, making conversation, which she was not very good at, which was why she avoided parties in the first place. She tried to think of a way to end this uncomfortable tête-à-tête. Looking around desperately – *There must be someone here who I know. After all, this is my neighbourhood!* – she was relieved to see the couple that ran the café next door to her shop. Even though she waved to them, Pedro tenaciously talked on.

"I hope to see you around, Bellísima," he ended, finally giving up.

"Yes, well maybe we'll run into each other again," she said as she walked quickly away from the table.

She found herself at the display case pushed up against the opposite wall. When her eyes focused and she actually looked at the contents, her pretended interest turned real. *Wow!*

She saw why Daniel had had difficulty describing the *objets*. There was no single category that could encompass everything here: a hand-painted rectangle of Thai silk backgrounded an ancient-looking clay figurine together with an ultra-sleek Italian coffee and teapot; a fat green jade Buddha laughed at a collection of Art Deco postcards; a Barbie doll dressed as an executive and carrying a brief case stood nose to nose with a tiny carved mask in the shape of a bird.

There were futuristic-looking robot figures and ancient-looking ceramic dishes.

The middle shelf was filled with hats and other head coverings: a large-brimmed neon pink straw hat half obscured a medieval-looking white wig which crowded up against a shiny black top hat next to an object – was it a hat? – that she couldn't identify: dazzling and colourful, a mass of yarn and feathers and shiny stones. As she stared in fascination, her mind arranged the parts and she found herself looking at – was it possible? – a Jewish yarmulka! Or something sort of like a yarmulka ... the same general shape at least ... but unlike any yarmulka she'd ever seen! "Is that a yarmulka?" "Yes," came the surprised answer, at which Bella realized she'd spoken out loud and that Zelda was standing next to her. "You're the first person to recognize it!"

"It's beautiful!"

"Thank you! I think so too."

"Did you make it?"

"Yes. I was very bored at a Bar Mitzvah and my imagination started playing with the ugly yarmulka in front of me. When I got home, I made this."

"It's gorgeous! Have you worn it?"

"Haven't had the chance yet ... I don't go to many Jewish events anymore."

"Me neither, but as it happens I have a baby thing soon," murmured Bella doubtfully, pretty sure that Avi's traditional family wouldn't approve of this head covering, "and it is sooo beautiful." Zelda had already turned to talk to another guest so, with a last covetous peek at the yarmulka, which she certainly didn't need for her very few Jewish occasions, Bella started towards the door. She looked for Daniel to say goodbye, couldn't see him anywhere and, not wanting to look too hard in case she found leering Pedro instead, left to do her grocery shopping.

She had just stepped out the door when she heard her name being called. She looked up and into a face she hadn't seen since leaving high school.

"Oh my god! Emkay!!" she cried as the other woman rushed towards her and they wrapped their arms around one another.

"Bel!! I haven't seen you in ages!!"

She and Emkay, known to her family and teachers as Marie-Christine, and to everyone else as MK, or Emkay, had spent many back row hours trying to make it through their last year of high school. Emkay's family had moved the summer before, and francophone Marie-Christine Fornay had ended up in Bella's English school through a combination of bureaucratic red tape, lost documents, changes in zone demarcations, and human error. By the time the mess was untangled, seven months had passed, so Emkay stayed where she was for the rest of the term. She and Bella had been inseparable all that year. After they'd both managed to scrape together enough marks to graduate and no longer met at school, they'd lost touch.

"Wow! Emkay! What are you doing here? Do you live around here?"

"I don't actually live anywhere. I've been in South America ever since I got divorced." She made a moue of disgust. "We won't talk about that mistake! South America's fantastic. I just came back because I ran out of money. I'm staying with my parents." She grimaced again. "We won't talk about that either. But just until I can get together enough money, and then I'm going back. How 'bout you?"

"I live here, around here, I have a store, a flower store."

"Oh! That's so … settled down! Who'd have thought?"

"Well, it has been a few years since high school …."

"I guess …. It's true, I tried the settled-down thing. Made my parents happy, they got to have their dream of a church-white-gown-wedding. Nice Catholic boy they approved of." She shivered. "Just the thought of it makes me sick! I can't believe I ever did that. Or that I stuck it out as long as I did!"

Bella remembered the Fournays: straight-laced traditional Catholics who did their best to close their eyes to everything she and Emkay were up to; Catholics who went to church every week and took their religion seriously. "How'd your folks feel about your divorce?"

Another scowl. "They were awful! That's one of the reasons I went traveling, to get away from them. I had nowhere else to live, so I was staying with them, and they just went on and on about it, how I was going to hell, especially as I wasn't going to confession anymore. Even for a free meal, I couldn't hack it anymore, so I left."

At the mention of food, Bella's stomach reminded her that she hadn't actually eaten yet, and that the snacks she'd consumed had been absorbed long ago. She needed to get on with her shopping.

"Are you around for a while? I have to go, but we could get together?" she asked, cutting into Emkay's bio-drama.

"Fab!! I'm only here 'til I can afford to go back, but that's not gonna happen right away."

Bella found a business card in her pocket and gave it to her high school buddy. "This is my store. Call or come by – we can catch up!"

∞

BY THE TIME EVERYONE LEFT, it was late; Daniel and Zelda collapsed onto the couch and breathed simultaneous sighs of relief.

"I'm so tired, I can't feel my feet!"

"I can't remember when I talked so much!"

They both laughed, then Zelda said, in a more serious voice, "But I think it went well, don't you?"

"It was a fun party," he agreed.

"And hopefully it will lead to actual customers."

"Well," he said, "we did all the right spells for that."

"Yes," she nodded, "let's hope the god and goddess are with us. They should be, we fed them well."

"Did you feed them tonight?" he asked suddenly.

"Yes, of course, before anyone came, I gave them some of everything. I think they especially liked the strawberries. I got them at the market, they were fresh picked this morning."

"I think everyone else liked them too! They went very quickly. As did those Spanish pastry things."

"Did you get any? Strawberries?" When her partner shook his head, she smiled wisely. "I thought that might happen so I put some aside for us. As soon as I can move, I'll go get them."

"Ah, you are truly a magnificent woman."

∞

OBJETS WAS CLOSED when Bella passed it the next morning, but the display cabinet was now in the window, and Zelda's beautiful yarmulka was even more eye-catching than it had been in the dim interior. The feathers were fluffed out into a kind of half-halo bordering the multicoloured crocheted cap on which various spots caught the light and glittered like diamonds. She admired it again, noting that it was so stunning in the daytime sunlight that it eclipsed the other objects in the window, beautiful and unique as they were.

She didn't understand why she was so drawn to it. Yes, it was beautiful; but she actually felt an urge to own it, which didn't happen often – her proprietary feeling about Belles Fleurs was a recurring surprise – and had never happened with anything remotely Jewish. Her Jewish heritage had always been a source of conflict for her. It was true that her negativity had toned down somewhat in the last few years. But still – wanting a yarmulka! Although this one really didn't look much like the traditional head covering, or at least what Bella had seen of them in her limited Jewish experiences. And, after all, Noemi had said she wanted non-traditional Jews to counterbalance Avi's relatives. They might not even recognize it and just think she was wearing a decorated hat. Well, there was no price tag on the yarmulka, or on any of the other objects, which probably meant she couldn't afford it anyway. She'd never had much money, and since she'd bought into the store last year, her disposable income had dwindled even more.

With her reduced finances in mind, she considered Belles Fleurs thoughtfully as she unlocked the door. Had it been a wise decision? She wished she could feel more secure and stop worrying and obsessing about it. It had been such a huge step for her, and it was only because her brother was helping that she'd managed to pay for her half. If her apartment hadn't been the smallest and cheapest on the block, she wouldn't have been able to afford to live by herself any more. Luckily, that crisis had been averted and she was still roommate-less, but kind of broke.

Stepping inside and looking around, she reaffirmed that, yes, it had been the right decision. She really did love her little shop. And, while it might never make her rich, it allowed her to live a life that she enjoyed. She loved the flowers that she spent so much time with. As she inhaled the fragrances that filled the store, she noticed a new scent. Excited, she twirled around to check and, sure enough, the jasmine flowers were now open. After making sure that she was completely and utterly alone, she sang her special song to them, the one she reserved for first times, but she kept the volume lower than usual. The incident with Daniel was still fresh, she didn't want a reprise of that mortification!

After having greeted her store and its inhabitants, she got to work; the beginning of the week was always the busiest. Besides being thirsty, the plants usually required a surprising amount of trimming, pruning, and general rearranging to show off their best sides to prospective customers. She was happily ensconced on the floor surrounded by orchids when she heard the door open. "Just a sec," she called out, "I'll be right there."

"Take your time, Bellísima. I like what I see!"

Her heart sank as she looked up to the same leer she had turned her back on the night before. Pasting on her professional smile, she stood up. "Pedro, is it?" At his nod, she added, "How nice to see you again. How did you find me?"

"I asked my good friend Daniel. When he told me about your beautiful little store, I just had to come and see." He looked around approvingly. "And it is, indeed, beautiful. Bellísima fleurs to go with a bellísima lady!"

"I'm actually a little busy right now." Bella was better at deflecting conversations in the store than at parties. "Did you want anything in particular?"

Totally unfazed, he grinned even more widely. "Not right now, but I'm sure I'll need something soon."

Not wanting to turn away potential business, even when it came in an unsavory form, Bella managed to swallow her irritation. "I look forward to that," she said evenly.

"Me too!"

∞

THE FOLLOWING EVENING, she just had to stop and admire the yarmulka again. She'd never felt this kind of attraction to any object: it actually seemed to be calling her name. She was very tempted to go inside and ask the price. *It couldn't hurt to ask, could it?* At least that way she'd know if it was way beyond her means. Her contemplation was inter-rupted when she felt a presence join her at the window. Not wanting to break the connection she felt with the yar-mulka, she kept her eyes firmly focused on it, hoping the interloper would leave, which hope was shattered when she heard the voice that had already become too familiar.

"That's mine. Do you like it?"

She followed the direction of Pedro's pointing finger to the shelf below the yarmulka.

"What's yours? The teapot?"

"That ugly shiny thing! No, no, the beautiful ancient Mayan figurine next to it. It is very old and very valuable."

Yes, it is lovely; but so is the modern teapot beside it, you arrogant little .... Luckily, the shop door opened before her irritation blossomed into words. And there was Daniel, wearing the grin she'd already come to associate with him.

"I was hoping you would come ...," he began and then stopped in surprise when he noticed Pedro standing beside her. Pedro showed no such hesitation. Clasping the hand that Daniel had stretched out towards Bella, he put his other arm around Daniel's shoulders. "Danny, my man! How are you?" Bella watched in admiration as Daniel ex-tracted himself elegantly.

"Good, Pedro, nice to see you."

"Great party the other night. Just thought I'd stop by and see how you folks are settling in."

"Yes, thank you, we even had a few customers today."

"Didn't sell my figurine yet, though, I see?"

"No, not yet," Daniel smiled tentatively, "it is not so cheap."

"No, of course not! It's a genuine artifact!"

The silence that followed was uncomfortable for Bella and, she thought, for Daniel, although maybe not for Pedro. She was about to extricate herself when Pedro waved in the general direction of Daniel, the store, and herself, said, "I'll see you," and took off.

The silence continued, but it already felt less burdensome. Bella turned to Daniel, who also seemed to be standing up straighter.

"Do you know Pedro well?" she asked.

"No, not well, just through the store. He brought us the figurine."

"Oh! He told me you were good friends."

"I think that is just the way he talks."

"He said you told him where to find me ...."

Daniel looked anxious. "Was that not right? He asked about you, so I told him about your store."

She hastened to reassure him, saying, "No, it's fine, it's not a secret, he could have found out from anyone in the neighbourhood."

"He is not bothering you?" Daniel still looked concerned.

"Nothing I can't handle." She smiled, wanting it to be true. "I was sorry not to say goodbye the other night, I didn't see you when I was leaving."

"Yes, so many people came!"

" I hope it's an auspicious beginning for your store."

"Me too," he said earnestly. "Zelda has put everything she has into it."

"Not you?"

"Yes, me too. But I did not have much. It is all her idea and her money ...."

"But you're partners?"

"Yes, yes, we are partners. But really it is her store, I just help her. We are in the same coven."

Bella was sure she must have misheard: "The same what?"

"Coven. You know, a Wiccan coven."

"Wiccan? You mean as in witches?"

"Well, yes. But the new version – the modern witches – we call ourselves Wiccans. I do not know all that much about it, I am just starting. Zelda has been a Wiccan for a long time, she can explain it better."

Okay, maybe this isn't as weird as it sounds. Witches in the middle of Montreal, why not? She remembered her brief conversation with Zelda, though, and asked, "But isn't she Jewish?"

"I think she still is, I am not sure, you have to ask her. It seems that you can be both."

Bella imagined what her firmly traditional Zaidy would have said about that. Or Avi's parents! Or, maybe Judaism was not always as limited as she'd believed?

"Well, it is a truly beautiful store," she said, gesturing towards the window.

"Yes, thank you, I think so too. We found many pieces and even made some ourselves. Zelda did the crochet, I did the masks."

"Oh!" Bella looked more closely at the bird mask gazing at executive Barbie. She'd been so entranced by the yarmulka, she hadn't looked at it carefully. Now she saw how precisely it was carved.

"Oh that's beautiful!" she exclaimed. "Is it a traditional design? From …?" She left the question unfinished as she had no idea what his background was, given his foreign accent and manners; also, her knowledge of any traditions, Canadian or other, was non-existent.

"No," he replied quickly, "I made it up."

A phone rang inside, and with an apologetic shrug of his shoulders, Daniel went to answer it.

∞

REALIZING THAT SHE'D forgotten to ask the price of the yarmulka, Bella stopped by again the next day. This time it was Zelda, sitting inside with her head bent over a ball of yarn, tending the store. "Hi!" Zelda greeted her. "So nice to see you again. I'm sorry, I've forgotten your name."

"Bella, from the flower store on the next block, Belles Fleurs."

"Oh yes, of course. There were so many people that night, so many faces ... and my memory's not as good as it used to be!" She laughed, pointing to her grey hair.

"I was admiring your yarmulka."

"Right, I remember now."

"Is that what you're working on now? Another one?"

"Yup," Zelda said, lifting up the yarn in her hands to show her.

Bella gave it a closer look. "Is it only yarmulkas you make?"

"Not only, but I've gotten into them recently. I think I told you I was at a boring Bar Mitzvah?" Bella nodded and she continued: "It was in Winnipeg, my niece's son's Bar Mitzvah. I don't usually go to these things, but my sister really wanted me there because our mother had just died, so I went. So there I was, bored out of my mind, sitting through the whole Saturday morning service, all three hours of it."

Bella nodded again. She was curious about Zelda's Jewish-Wiccan combination but was shy to ask. She didn't like people knowing her personal business and she assumed everyone else felt the same, unless they told her differently. It wasn't even Zelda who had told her about the witchy stuff. Maybe it was a secret. So she didn't want to come right out and ask. Zelda didn't seem to be like her, though, as she continued exposing her private life to a stranger:

"I needed something to keep my eyes open, so I focused on the head in front of me. Which was wearing one of those tacky ugly yarmulkas with the Bar Mitzvah boy's name. I had really gotten into crocheting and started fantasizing about the ugly yarmulka, thinking about what I could do to transform it into an object of beauty, into something even I would wear! When I got back home, I started playing with the ideas, experimenting and trying things, and this is what I came up with. The one in the window was my first."

That reminded Bella of her reason for entering the store. "Yes it's so amazing – I keep looking at it every time I go by. How much is it?" she asked before she could stop herself.

"Sorry, it's not for sale. I like it too much, I need to keep it." Seeing Bella's disappointed look, she added, "But I can make you one. I can't guarantee exactly how it will end up, they're all different. You tell me what you like, I do my thing, and you only have to take it if you want it."

While Bella liked the sound of that, she still needed to know what it would cost before she could agree. Zelda brushed the question away: "We'll talk about that later. The more important question is what you like." Bella wasn't sure that was true, but she wouldn't be actually committing herself. So they talked colours and designs, feathers, beads, sequins, and crystals until Bella's head was spinning with possibilities.

"I'll put that all in my head and see what comes out," Zelda promised. "Just as soon as I finish this one, which is already spoken for."

Bella, in turn, agreed to think about it, still unsure if she was ready to welcome a yarmulka into her life at any price.

∞

"WHAT? No dancing? No singing?"

She spun around to face the wide smile in the doorway. Although still sensitive about their first encounter, she was happy to see Daniel and not Pedro.

"No, that was a one-time-only performance!" She laughed self-consciously. "In fact, you're the only person to have ever seen it!"

"I am the lucky one then. I should have taken a picture, I could have sold it on eBay…"

"Ha, ha," she laughed with him, but her laughter was more forced, especially when he added, "… or uploaded it to YouTube!"

"Thank god, you didn't," she shuddered.

"I have some pictures. Not of you," he quickly added when she flinched, "of pieces that Zelda made." He brought a large brown envelope over to her desk. "She asked me to bring them to you. You ladies were talking?"

"Yes, I stopped in yesterday and we talked about her yarmulkas. They are so beautiful!"

"Are you going to have one?"

"I'm thinking about it …."

"How about a mask as well? You could put it up in here."

"Do you do custom work too?"

"I haven't so far, but no one has expressed the interest."

"The one in the window is beautiful, I've never seen any quite like it. Is it traditional?" *Great, I sound like an idiot tape recorder on rewind. What is it about this man that I can't talk to him like a normal person?*

"No, not traditional," he answered hurriedly. "Well, I don't want to get in your way, I know you have things to do. See you later." And, with another flash of his smile, he left.

He must think I'm a total moron, guess I won't be seeing too much of him.

Still, in case he did show up again, she resolved to tone down her morning greetings even more, to start whispering hello to the plants and refrain from spinning. "It's not you," she hastened to reassure her audience. "I just don't want this showing up on the Internet!" From the corner of her eye, she caught an understanding wink from the bright orange hibiscus by the door, although it might just have been the petals fluttering in the morning breeze.

∞

IT WAS ANOTHER hot humid summer-in-Montreal day and the Noemi who appeared in the early afternoon looked ready to collapse. Bella rushed to guide her to a seat and hovered worriedly, asking, "Do you need anything? To drink? Water? Juice? To put your feet up?" Noemi had closed her eyes as soon as she sat down, but opened them now and tried to smile: "Water please."

"What are you doing out on a day like this? Especially in the middle of the day?" Bella chided as she handed over the tall glass of cold water, which the pregnant woman held against her forehead for a moment before gulping down the contents.

Noemi let out a huge sigh and a burp. "Oops, excuse me. I don't seem to have much control over my body anymore!" She held out the glass for a refill. When Bella brought it, she smiled sheepishly, saying, "Thanks. I needed to get out, I go stir crazy at home. And walking seems to lull this baby to sleep. It's just a little too hot."

When they were interrupted by a customer, Noemi gazed pleadingly at Bella: "Do you mind if I hang out here for a while? You don't have to take any notice or even talk, I just want to rest."

"Sure, no problem."

Bella went off to serve the customer, who was enchanted by the jasmine flowers he'd glimpsed through the window. He was even more thrilled when he smelled the delicate white blossoms. By the time Bella had finished telling him about the plant, its history, and its requirements, he'd made up his mind to buy both. Bella was sad to see them go, she hadn't had a chance to really enjoy them, but pleased to have made such a lucrative sale. Bidding them farewell, she helped him carry them to the van outside. She'd just gotten back to her desk and sat down beside Noemi's slumbering body when Daniel, preceded as usual by his smile, walked in holding the brown envelope.

"I forgot to leave the pictures this morning."

"Oh right!" Maybe he didn't think she was a total idiot. Or maybe Zelda had made him come back. At the sound of his voice, Noemi opened her eyes and, seeing his huge grin, smiled immediately in return.

"Hello there! I didn't mean to wake you."

"I wasn't really sleeping, just resting this ... this ...," she said, indicating her large belly.

"It looks heavy," he sympathized.

"And how!" Bella was glad to see her laugh, seemingly refreshed by her nap.

"What's in the envelope?" Noemi wanted to know.

"Yarmulka pictures." Bella handed it to her.

"Yarmulkas? What's that?" Noemi was already opening the envelope to see for herself.

"You know, Jewish head coverings." She made a circle around her head to illustrate her meaning.

"Oh – you mean kippahs!" At Bella's blank look, she went on, "That's what I've always heard them called. Maybe it's a Hebrew thing." By now, she'd opened the envelope and was looking at the pictures of crocheted kippahs/yarmulkas. "What do you want to see these for?"

"Daniel's partner makes them," Bella explained. "You remember, the new store that had its opening last week?"

Noemi shook her head. "No. Did you tell me about it?"

"You saw the poster. For the opening."

"Oh, maybe .... I think this baby's scrambling my memory along with everything else." She smiled at Daniel and stuck out her hand, saying, "Hi, I'm Noemi, Bella's pregnant friend. I would get up but I can't."

"No, no, please do not even think of it. Pregnant ladies should be waited on," he said as he took her hand and brought it up to his lips, just as he'd done with Bella the other night.

"I like this man! Can I introduce him to Avi? My husband," she explained, turning back to Daniel.

"I would be honoured. And he will see how to appreciate such a beautiful woman as yourself," was the gallant response.

"Better and better!" Noemi exclaimed. "Maybe I can even trade him in! Are you single?"

"Indeed I am," he answered.

Bella looked up from the catalogue of locally-grown tropical plants she'd turned to when her visitors started their conversation. "I thought Zelda was your partner."

"Oh, no, she is so old!" He clapped his hand over his mouth when he realized how that sounded and immediately tried to explain it away: "I mean, she is not so old, not really, but she is somewhat older than me…." He stopped bothering when he saw the two women laughing at him.

"Didn't you say she was your partner?" Bella asked.

"Yes, she is my business partner. And we are friends. But no more than that!" He shook his head in emphasis.

Noemi was still in a teasing mood as she continued to grill Daniel: "Well, I'm glad we got that cleared up! What about the rest of your life?"

Bella took the catalogue and phone into the backroom, glad that Noemi had found someone to talk to. She didn't mind her coming into the store, but had neither time nor inclination for prolonged chats. The sound of their voices became a background murmur as she concentrated on her ordering.

She was trying to utilize local sources for exotics. When she'd first started working at Belles Fleurs, their business was mostly in cut flowers, mostly imported from warmer countries. Over the years she, along with many of their customers, had become aware of and concerned about the environmental cost of the imported flowers, the large ecological footprint created by their watering, growing, and shipping requirements. Now, whenever local growers offered tropical plants grown in nearby hothouses, she sampled their products and, if they were up to her standards, turned to them for her supplies.

The nature of the business had also changed. Cut flowers used to account for almost all their sales. These were still significant, especially at Valentine's and Mother's Days, but more and more people preferred potted flowering plants, which could produce blossoms again if cared for properly.

She'd been excited to receive this catalogue from a new grower who'd set up just east of Montreal. Among their first offerings were bromeliads and Brazilian fireworks, neither of which she'd been able to find previously. She ordered two of each: enough to allow for individual variations, but few enough that she could afford to lose her investment if the plants were either unhealthy or didn't sell. Jean-Pierre had taught her how to ease into new producers and new products.

While she was in ordering mode, she also put in a request to the jasmine supplier, for six plants this time, because of her customer's response and because she herself had also loved the look and smell of the small bushes. Satisfied with her choices, she returned to the front of the shop, where she overheard Noemi asking Daniel where he was from.

"I can't place your accent, but I think you're not from here. And I guess you can tell I'm not either. I'm from

North Africa, Morocco. How about you?" Interested in hearing his reply, Bella stopped and listened.

"Oh, here and there," he smiled charmingly, "mostly there."

Her phone rang at that moment and Bella went back to the quiet storeroom to answer it. She returned to serve a customer who appeared shortly thereafter. The afternoon got busy. Between that customer and the succession of people who came in to buy or browse, the day slipped by. She barely had time to nod goodbye to Daniel when he left. She didn't notice Noemi's exit at all.

When she had a minute to herself again, she sat down to rest her feet and took a look at the pictures Zelda had sent. Along with the hard copies was a note saying she had just created an online portfolio with a website address (Ed. note: For Zelda's portfolio, see http://zeldamoon-star.crevado.com). *Wow, wow and more wow!* Besides photographs of yarmulkas, there were jewelry, bags, clothing, and wall hangings. Even among the yarmulkas, each one was unique: different colours and patterns, each decorated with an assortment of beads, feathers, stones, sequins and things she couldn't identify. Each was striking, rich with its own personality. *What a gift she has to be able to create these.* She didn't know much about art, but she knew this was something more than just 'craft' and, therefore, almost certainly out of her price range. There was no price list included with the pictures. And Zelda had still not mentioned an amount. *Not a good sign.*

∞

FROM THE VERY BEGINNING, Bella had had to reconcile herself to the shop being a people-magnet; she understood it as a business asset and tried not to mind. That was business. It was the strictly social part she had trouble with. The problem was that people knew where to find her and felt they could just sashay into her work place and monopolize her time. Sometimes, especially when she was working alone in the store and people wanted to chat, her small amount of socializing-ability was pushed to its limit. She was beginning to feel like Belles Fleurs had been transformed into Grand Central Station, with people dropping in and out like commuter trains.

Daniel and Pedro both became part of her daily routine. Daniel didn't always come in, but he tapped on the window and flashed her a smile as he waved and went by. After just a few days, the sight had become so familiar she hardly noticed it anymore.

Pedro, on the other hand, almost always came in, although he didn't stay long. Just enough to irritate her. Maybe he thought he'd wear her down; certainly her tepid responses had had no discernible effect on him.

This morning Zelda came by as well. It was her first visit and it took her a long time to get around to her purpose because she was so excited by the flowers. She inspected them, smelling and admiring; she was especially captivated by the bromeliad which had arrived that morning. She knew about plants, that was obvious from her questions and comments; she was pleased when Bella told her the bromeliad was local. When she'd finished her tour, she seemed to realize how long she'd been there.

"Sorry to take up so much of your time," she apologized. "I got distracted by your beautiful flowers! I really just came in to make sure Daniel brought you the pictures of my crocheting."

Bella had been so caught up in Zelda's passion that she didn't try to tone down her own delight in the crocheted pieces. Zelda, in turn, was so touched by Bella's reaction that tears appeared in her eyes. Bella was reluctant to bring up the question of money at that point, it seemed too crass.

Before she could figure out how to broach the subject, Zelda had gone.

Pedro dropped by, although, thankfully, he seemed on his way somewhere, because he only stayed long enough to embrace her unwilling body and plant a kiss on her unresponsive cheek, then he was gone.

Emkay stopped by shortly after, also on her way elsewhere, planted the Montreal two-cheek kisses on a much more willing face, gave a cursory glance around the store which finished with an ambiguous grunt, and arranged to meet for dinner the following Tuesday, then she too was gone.

Daniel came in about an hour later, also staying for a very short time. "Just checking up on one of my favourite ladies." She'd realized that his gallant tone was not personal, that this was his usual manner.

Noemi showed up in the early afternoon and sank into 'her' chair while Bella was explaining the intricate watering process for the delicate purple orchid a teenage boy was buying for his mother. "Do you want me to write it down?" she asked, but he shook his head. "No, I can look it up on the internet if I need to."

After he left holding his fragile package carefully, Bella rearranged the orchids on display so that the remaining purple flower was in front.

"Those are so lovely." Bella had forgotten Noemi was there and gave a small start when she heard her voice. Noemi was an undemanding visitor, but liked to talk if Bella was up for it.

"Something to drink?" she asked and, at Noemi's nod, brought her some cold juice.

"Anything new?" she inquired as she sat down

"Just the same old same old. Aching feet, sore back, too hot, too tired, avoiding the circumcision discussion because it gives me heartburn." She pulled a face. "Unfortunately, that one's not going to go away like the aching feet."

They sat for a few moments in silence.

"He was nice," Noemi said suddenly. At Bella's questioning look, she elaborated: "Daniel."

"You two seemed to be getting on well."

"It was fun to talk to someone new!"

"And he is charming," Bella observed drily.

"Isn't he just! Good looking too."

Bella nodded her agreement.

"Where's he from?" Noemi asked. "I asked him but he didn't really answer. His English is better than his French, but I can't place his accent in either one."

"I don't know," Bella shrugged. "I've just met him a couple of times."

"Those kippahs his partner makes? They look beautiful!"

"They're incredible. I'm thinking of getting one."

"Really? A kippah? What for?"

"I'm not sure," she said, too embarrassed to tell Noemi that it seemed to be calling to her. "I haven't decided yet."

"It must be all this circumcision talk that's getting to you. You're getting ready for the baby ritual!"

"Maybe that's it. After all, I'll need something to wear!"

Week 3

Another period of relative calm allowed them to resume their normal, or as close to normal as possible, lives. He even went to school sometimes, although this depended on whether the roads were safe enough for him, and for the teacher, to reach the bombed-out shell that had once been a school. The only supplies they had were the few pencils and books the teacher managed to scavenge. He started to take his brother with him, so he could also get an education, minimal as it was. His parents were insistent; they believed the war could not last forever and, when it ended, they wanted their sons better off than they'd been on their subsistence farm.

They were both at school the day their parents died. The roads had been passable and quiet in the early morning, but the afternoon brought renewed fighting, much more fierce than anything he could remember. There were no tanks or planes this time, but so many men running through streets and into houses, shouting and shooting.

The teacher wouldn't let any of the children leave. She gathered them all in an underground chamber they'd created for this contingency, then covered them with straw, after cautioning them to stay absolutely quiet until she came back. She never did come back. They crept out of their refuge the next morning, into a world of stillness and silence.

When he got home, carrying his brother, who had maintained his terrified muteness, they found their father's body, bloody and battered, inside the house. They didn't find their mother until the next day, a few streets over, in a pile of dead women.

Not knowing what else to do, he stood in his doorway, choking as the sobs racked his entire body and being, his brother close beside him also weeping, but silently. The woman who lived next door, whose family had managed to survive the slaughter somehow, came over and led them, by the hands, into her own house.

∞

DANIEL HAD BEGUN to feel a proprietary pride in the neighbourhood, the street, and the store. He loved swinging down 'his' street, on the way to 'his' store, waving hello to his new neighbours, flashing the large smile that expressed the joy bubbling up inside him. When he crossed the threshold into *objets*, he found himself performing a greeting similar to the one he'd seen Bella doing the day they met. He imagined the inanimate subjects of his own kingdom waking up, shaking off sleep, and donning their best appearance for customers.

He had a complete morning routine. He and Zelda had sanctified the store before opening, and they reinforced the sacrality each day with blessings, incantations, and offerings. Each morning, Daniel started in the north corner, where he greeted and thanked the earth spirit for its presence and protection. He then continued clockwise, stopping in the east to greet the spirit of air, the south for fire, and the west for water. Then he moved to the altar in the centre, where he topped up the bowl of salt for the earth, lit a new stick of incense for air, lit the fiery candle, and replenished the bowl of water: rites to honour the Wiccan deities, as Zelda had taught him, but also strangely reminiscent of ceremonies and spirits he had grown up with. The next part he'd added himself, after witnessing Bella's exuberant greeting. He spun around, arms rising with each turn until they were straight out at shoulder height. He allowed them to sweep him around, bringing everything in the store into one embrace, after which he folded his arms inwards, crossing them over his heart as he gave a final thanks to the universe for bestowing this gift on him.

Only then, when he was satisfied that the inside space was ready to greet the world, did he actually unlock the door, switch on the lights, and flip the sign to '*open.*' He made himself coffee and settled down to his daily tasks: dusting, bookkeeping, phone and mail, and, if any time was left over, working on his carvings. He often spent the entire day at the store; Zelda was not so good at being punctual or keeping regular hours. He had no problem with this, it was his contribution to their partnership. She had put up all the money as he had none, and he did most of the daily management. It was an arrangement that suited them both very well.

∞

"So, BEL, what have you been up to?"

Bella gestured around her in response to Emkay's question: "This is my life, pretty well has been all these years." Before she could get depressed about how boring she sounded, she asked quickly, "What about you? What have you been doing?"

"Well, I tried the whole parents' dream thing. Got married, to a nice enough guy, moved to Brossard, had three miscarriages, decided my life was meaningless, and split!"

Bella couldn't help laughing, this was the Emkay she remembered. "But what made you try it in the first place?"

"I have no idea, when I think about it now. At the time, it seemed like a good idea. But then again, I think I may have been too high to really think about it. Those years in Brossard were a total fog."

"What kind of high were you on – in Brossard!" This was accompanied by the sneer inner-city dwellers reserve for the suburbs.

"Don't knock it," was the response. "Everything you could possibly want, delivered right to your door, day or night! I was into tranqs at the time, with chasers of booze .... I think I slept through those years. Finally woke up enough to get the hell out of there!"

While Bella ran around closing up the store, Emkay sat and twiddled her thumbs, waiting for her to be ready, then sprang to her feet, saying, "Let's go!"

As they passed *objets*, Bella asked her old friend, "How do you know Zelda and Daniel?"

"Who?"

"The people whose store this is, where we bumped into each other? At the opening?"

"Oh, right! I don't know them, I just met some people who were going and it sounded like fun, so I tagged along."

Over dinner, they had drinks and more drinks while Emkay regaled her with stories about her life. It had been a long time since Bella'd drunk so much and she switched to soda when she realized it. Emkay stayed with the wine, she didn't even seem to notice. What an exciting life she'd led, so many places and people, so many adventures. At first Bella was envious, it made her own life sound so tame, so lame. After a while, though, she realized she was getting worn out just hearing about it. Emkay's stories all blended into one and, by the end of the evening, Bella was bored.

She didn't feel too well when she woke up the next morning. Her headache reminded her of last year's poisoned latkes, but when she stood up and took a few steps, she realized it was a hangover. *As long as I don't move my head too much I should be ok.* She walked to work more carefully than usual, sank into her chair, and drank two cups of black coffee.

That's it! I am never doing that again. She was sure she saw a thumbs up from the hibiscus in the corner. *Yes you're right my dear. Definitely time to get started.* She dragged herself up to get the watering can.

∞

WHEN SHE CAME IN that afternoon, Noemi looked totally dejected.

"What's wrong?" Bella put down her pruning shears.

Noemi tried to wave away the gloom that enveloped her. "Sorry, sorry, I tried to not bring my bad mood with me."

"What is it? Is something wrong with the baby?"

"No, no, he's fine. At least, I hope he is!" She stopped for a moment as the possibility of the baby not being okay hit her. Then she brushed it away. "No, it's this stupid circumcision thing again, which just will not go away! Now Avi's sister is here and they're both on at me about the *brit milah*."

"The what?"

"The circumcision. Even though Nurit is not the slightest bit religious. They both seem to think it will kill their parents if we don't do it. I'm so tired of arguing about it! If I'd known this would happen, I'd have aborted it!" At Bella's gasp, she smiled ruefully: "I don't really mean that. Or maybe I do! I don't know anymore. All I know is that this is awful and I don't know how we will resolve it! I can't bear the thought of mutilating my precious new-born tiny helpless baby that I've carried so carefully for nine months. And Avi can't seem to bear the thought of not going through with what he insists on calling the 'absolute Jewish requirement'." Noemi closed her mouth and her eyes, in complete rejection of Avi's perspective.

Noemi's frustration reinforced Bella's opinion that, for the most part, relationships were more trouble than they were worth. Distracted by the thought, she forgot about Noemi and drifted off: at least she could make her own decisions without having to compromise, about her personal life at any rate, she amended, remembering that she co-owned the store. Although, so far, Jean-Pierre and Carl had been happy to leave all the managing in her hands. She got to make the decisions, such as bringing in the bromeliads. She would have to wait to see if that turned out to be a good decision or not. If they sold, she would order more.

But she wasn't sure about the nursery they came from, the Brazilian Fireworks looked a little droopy. She suspected they'd been forced to grow too fast, often a problem with hothouse set-ups, especially the new ones. The downside to all the decision-making being on her shoulders was her constant worrying which, she hoped, experience would eventually eliminate.

In the back room, checking her stock of plant food, she heard the door chime and poked her head into the shop. Her nostrils were assailed by the fragrant smell that had enticed her to brave *objets'* opening party. She saw Pedro taking the lid off a plastic container in front of Noemi, who seemed mesmerized by the pupusas. Bella got to them just as Noemi picked one up and popped it into her mouth. At the first taste, she closed her eyes and moaned apprecia-tively.

"Oh mmm, that is good!" she finally said when her mouth was free.

Pedro grinned at Bella. "You see? You are not the only one to enjoy my mother's cooking!" he crowed.

Noemi turned to her. "You've tasted these?"

Bella nodded and couldn't help but smile at her friend's enthusiasm. "I have indeed."

"Bellísima, you must introduce me to your appreciative friend!" She winced – she was going to have to tell him not to call her by that name. Not only was the joke getting stale, the only other people who'd ever used it were the monsters she'd endured in high school, and those were not memo-ries she cared to relive. But her desire to avoid confronta-tion kept the smile pasted on her face while she performed the introductions: "Noemi, Pedro."

At least he didn't hold on to Noemi's hand while his eyes swept over her body. Perhaps her pregnant belly dis-couraged him. Noemi just turned back to the pupusas and took another one. "These are incredible! What are they called again?"

"Pupusas." At her questioning look, he elaborated: "From El Salvador; my mother makes them." He turned to Bella. "She made these for you."

"Why would she do that?" The question was out of her mouth before she could frame it more politely.

"You told me to thank her, remember?"

"Oh yes, I did," she granted, remembering her response to the first taste of the pastries, before he'd said enough for her to stop being polite.

"So I did, and she made these for you! I told her you were bellísima and about your bellísima store."

Bella remembered her manners, just in time, as well as the fact that she couldn't afford to ignore potential business. She turned to the orchids she had arranged that morning and picked out a small but lovely red-flowered plant. "You must give her this for me," she said, handing it to him. "Please thank her again."

"Perhaps you will get the chance to thank her yourself one of these days." He had not released her hand after taking the plant and squeezed it now.

Bella slipped back into her cool manner as she tried to subtly extricate her hand. "Yes, perhaps." She looked at Noemi for help, but her pregnant friend had already closed her eyes again.

"Perhaps we could have dinner," Pedro continued, still holding fast to her hand.

She tugged a little harder, freed her hand and stepped back. "I don't think so."

The entrance of another customer saved her from having to continue this awkward conversation. She resolutely kept her glance elsewhere while she tended to her customer, and then to the others who came in. By the time she had to go over to the desk, both Pedro and Noemi had gone, only the dish of pupusas remained.

∞

MATHIEU SHOWED UP on Friday. "What are you doing here?" a surprised Bella asked her downstairs neighbour. "I thought you were away for a few more days."

He shrugged. "I was with my family, it was enough. There's nothing to do in the country."

She began to show him all the new stock she'd acquired while he was away. He was especially taken with the bromeliads, as she'd known he would be. Mathieu was an avid gardener who kept the tiny space between their building and the sidewalk filled with colourful blooms all summer. He admired the hibiscus and was sorry he'd missed the jasmine flowers – the buds had appeared before he'd left and he'd been looking forward to seeing, and smelling, the actual blossoms. He was happy to hear she'd ordered more.

They'd just sat down when Noemi came in with a short thin woman who looked even thinner by contrast. Mathieu jumped up from the chair and offered it to a grateful Noemi, who beckoned to her companion. "This is my sister-in-law, Nurit. Nurit, these are my friends Bella and Mathieu."

Bella stood up, wondering if she was going to have to invest in more chairs for all these visitors. She was rescued from socializing by the ringing phone. Grabbing it, she moved into the storeroom to answer. When she got back, Noemi was in her usual closed-eyes half-asleep posture. Mathieu and Nurit were browsing among the tropical plants.

Bella brought Noemi a glass of water and sat down next to her. The pregnant woman opened one eye and took the glass with a grateful exhalation. "I hope you don't mind my bringing her, I didn't know what else to do with her. Avi's at work." She looked towards her sister-in-law, deep in conversation with Mathieu, and said hopefully, "Maybe Mathieu could entertain her?"

"Don't you like her?"

"She's okay. But we don't have much in common and I'm not up to making the effort right now and I really, really don't want to talk about circumcision!"

"Are her parents here as well?"

"No, they live in Israel. She's studying in England, so she came a few weeks early. I think she thought it would be fun here, but she doesn't know anyone except us."

She took a deep drink from the glass, then held it against her forehead. "I am so tired of being hot and cranky!" She took another swig and put down the empty glass. "What's with that Pedro guy? Is he after you or what?"

"I hope not!"

"At least if you marry him, you'll have a great cook for a mother-in-law. Those pupusas were delicious."

"Don't even joke about the possibility!" Bella responded with a shudder. As she finished saying this, Nurit and Mathieu came back to the desk, both smiling and chattering in French.

"This is great," Nurit said. "I don't get a chance to speak French much anymore, with being either in England or Israel. Noemi, if you don't mind, Mathieu offered to show me around the city."

"No problem," Noemi said, "no problem at all."

∞

THIS WAS THE perfect way to spend the day. Mathieu had been so glad to be back in the city that he'd almost kissed the sidewalk after getting off the bus. Showing it off to a visitor meant he could spend the day revisiting some of his favourite places.

He loved his family, he really did, but had always found the little town where he'd grown up, and where his parents and grandmother still lived, way too limited, offering none of the amenities that appealed to him. From a young age, he'd loved comics and games and all things related. This love had increased as he grew up and he was still a passionate gamer, spending much of his leisure time as an online avatar. This was not an activity that held the slightest interest for anyone else in his family. They'd embraced his ex-wife, undoubtedly thinking she would help ground him in reality. But that hadn't happened. In fact, her last words to him had been: "Grow up! You're not a child any longer, stop acting like one!"

Neither he nor his family had changed. Much as he loved them, it was difficult to spend any time there. After he finished catching up on the doings of his siblings and assorted cousins, there was nothing left to talk about. And his grandmother, bless her heart, was obsessed with finding him another wife. He suspected that she'd never forgiven him for the breakup, not to mention the divorce, which totally offended her Catholic soul. She kept trying to fix him up with every available unmarried woman. It wasn't that he didn't want to find a girlfriend (although he wasn't sure about a new wife), but he'd yet to find any female who shared his interests in games, comics, or even silly movies. His *grand-mère* understood that he liked the city and what it offered, so she tried to find him urban women. But, so far at least, they had all been into art and opera and theatre. And 'high' culture bored him beyond the point where he could even pretend interest.

The town, really more of a village, didn't offer much in the way of distractions. The first week they'd spent in the nearby 'city', immersed in all the pre-, during- and post-wedding activities of his cousin. Then he'd returned with his parents and grandmother to their hometown. And he'd been totally bored. He couldn't even get any service for his phone. So, when he had to get away, all he could do was go for long walks, either by himself or with the dog. He didn't mind doing this once or twice, but after two days, he'd reached his limit. So he made an excuse to his unsurprised parents and came home, after promising Grand-maman he would look up the niece of the neighbour's brother's wife, who was single and lived in the city.

He was so glad to be back that he couldn't sit still. He dropped off his bag and reunited with his cat, who initially ignored him, angry at his long absence, but forgave him as soon as a bowl of tuna was offered. Then he needed to get out, to walk somewhere where there were actually things to SEE, not just trees and birds! He drank in the fragrance and revelled in the sounds of traffic: all evidence of people with things to do and places to go.

He dropped in to see his neighbour Bella at her store, to say hello and tell her he was back. She'd been feeding and spending time with his cat, for which he was very grateful. He would have brought her a token of his gratitude, but had found nothing remotely acceptable.

Meeting Nurit was an unexpected treat. He liked Noemi: she shared his interest in graphic novels, had even spent a day looking at his collection with Fritz purring on her lap, which had endeared her to man and cat for life. Even if she found most of his action comics not to her taste, she was already a major improvement over every other woman he'd ever met. Too bad she seemed to be happily married, and her growing belly was an unmistakable sign of her unavailability.

How wonderful would it be if her sister-in-law shared that interest. Maybe Moroccan women were different from Canadian ones? She wasn't hard to look at and was around his age. Both her English and French had an accent that he couldn't place. "That's the Hebrew," she'd explained. "My parents are from Morocco, I was born in Israel. I learned my French from Israeli Moroccans."

She oohed and aahed at all the right places as they explored the city. By the time they got back to his neighbourhood, Mathieu was so delighted that he was working up to inviting her over to meet Fritz. They were still a couple of blocks away from his home when he noticed something unexpected.

"Oh," he exclaimed, "a new store! That's wonderful. This hasn't been a great block, so many abandoned businesses. Let's go look." As he pointed at *objets*, a tall figure came out, locked the door, and hurried off in the opposite direction. "Ah, that's too bad, it's closed now. But we can still look at the window."

He reached for Nurit's arm to cross the street but stopped, sensing movement in the shadows behind them. He frowned as he stared into the dark alley, at the two figures moving furtively apart and scurrying off. As director of the local neighbourhood watch, he had been actively involved in the cleanup two years before that had made their little *quartier* drug free. Ongoing vigilance had managed to keep it that way and Mathieu was upset at what looked like a possible resurgence of the problem. Unsure of what he'd seen, he appealed to Nurit for a second opinion. "Did you see that?" he asked, before realizing she was no longer there.

He found her on the other side of the street, in front of the new store. "I was talking to empty air...," he started, in mock outrage. His humour was wasted, she wasn't listening. She seemed totally focused on the street down which the tall figure had retreated. Mathieu scrutinized the area, but could see nothing. "What are you looking at?" he asked. "Nurit?" He touched her shoulder to get her attention. "Nurit?" he asked again. She returned to him, then, and shrugged. "Nothing," she answered, "I just thought I saw something."

"Me too, but across the street! Isn't that weird? Guess we're both seeing things," he laughed.

They turned to look at the store window. Mathieu got excited when he saw the Transformer action figure and even more so when he caught sight of the executive Barbie doll. He was enthusiastically babbling on about both of these when he realized he'd lost his audience again. Nurit was still gazing into the distance. She swiveled toward him when he touched her shoulder again, saying, "Are you okay?"

"Yes, yes, I'm fine!" She looked at the window. "Yes, isn't this stuff great! Just great!"

In wholehearted agreement, he resumed his animated commentary. This time he noticed the middle shelf with its cluster of head coverings. "Great hats! Look at that sparkly hat-thing," he said, indicating the yarmulka. He was engrossed in identifying its elements when he felt her suddenly clutch his arm and gasp.

This definitely didn't seem okay. "What's the matter? Are you alright?" he asked, alarmed.

"Yes, no, yes. A bit dizzy, but I'm fine. It's just … it's just … I just remembered I promised Noemi I'd be back soon. Thank you so much for a lovely day," she said, recovering quickly. And, before he could answer, she'd run off, leaving a somewhat astounded Mathieu staring after her open-mouthed.

Yah, sure, she 'just remembered,' as if. She didn't have to put on such a big show. She could have just said if she was bored and didn't want to see me again, he muttered internally, as he traipsed home confused and dejected.

Week 4

They stayed with the neighbours. His brother had such a sweet and gentle disposition that everyone loved him. He turned even more vigorously to his studies, he knew that's what his parents would have wanted. And they'd been right, the war did end one day. Except for occasional visits from the neighbour's brother, who was still off fighting in the south, their lives became more normal, more calm.

Now that the government didn't have to spend all its money on the war, it started extracting oil from underground, and the country began to climb out of its abyss. Roads needed to transport oil were repaired or built, schools needed to educate workers were repaired and stocked with supplies. Houses, stores, even hotels for foreign workers appeared. Slowly, the ruined city gained a semblance of life.

He began to allow himself moments of imagining a future when he and his brother could live, safe and secure, with enough to eat and with no one threatening their lives.

∞

"For chrissakes, this has got to be the worst job ever. If I have to stay here one more minute, I swear I'll go fucking crazy. There is nothing here. There will never be anything here. This place is dead. Dead, dead, dead! They're fucking crazy if they think he's coming fucking back. Especially in the fucking night. It's been way too fucking long already, he's obviously not fucking coming."

He had started speaking out loud just to keep himself awake. He was squeezed into the shadow of the abandoned building, had been there for what felt like forever already, although he knew from looking at the time on his phone that it was only 2:00 a.m. He'd been there eight hours the night before. Then, after the boss's much shorter shift, it was his turn again. And he'd made it clear he was to stay … until. "Until what?" he'd asked. "When do we give this up as useless?" "Until I say so," had been the very clear answer.

That was 6 hours ago. Six very long hours ago. He'd had enough. *Time to show some initiative, to show them what I'm capable of. Not just fucking boring no-action jobs, but real work. I'll show them! Then they'll see. Maybe even promote me, so I can give the orders! Ha! See how the big fucker likes that!*

The more he thought about it, the more he liked the idea. He'd been working for them for months and they'd yet to let him figure anything out himself, because they'd never seen what he was capable of. The big fucker bossing him around was probably responsible for that, telling them he wasn't ready. What did he know? He'd never given him a fucking chance!

He looked across the street, where, even from this distance and in the dim light from the window, the diamonds sparkled. *What are we waiting for? The diamonds are what we want! The guy's obviously a no-show, obviously long gone by now.* But the diamonds were there, sparkling, waiting … waiting for him to grab them ….

He was in the middle of the road when he saw them. *Shit shit shit!* Hidden by the overhang of the building next door, they'd been invisible. *Maybe they can't see me either?* One slunk away without looking back, but the other glanced up as he reached the sidewalk.

∞

AT LAST! The deserted warehouse came into sight. He'd phoned the boss with the code for *Got it*, which meant meeting as soon as possible. He'd done his best, but it hadn't been easy. He'd made sure to stay invisible, and navigating the unfamiliar city in the dark without asking directions had resulted in him getting lost a few times, so it had taken a while. But he was sure, once the boss saw the diamonds, he'd not only be forgiven, but commended for his smarts and his get-up-and-go!

He ran the last stretch and burst into the building, eager to show off his enthusiasm and dedication. The boss was there, tapping his foot ominously. Not known for his understanding or tolerance, the hours of delay had used up whatever patience the bigger man possessed. He decided not to bother with excuses or explanation, just go for the gold! Triumphantly, he pulled the yarmulka out of his pocket. And waited. But the other man just stared at his outstretched hand while his scowl deepened.

"What the fuck is this?" he growled at last.

The other's triumphant smile faltered. "It's the diamonds! I decided we should just grab …"

"The hell it is!" Snatching it at last, he held the yarmulka closer to his face for a moment staring at the largest of the glittery stones. "You idiot!" he cried. "You fucking fuck-up stupid fucking moron! Does this look like a diamond to you?"

The shorter man took a step back from the other's fury, trying to justify his initiative. "It's what you said," he managed to stammer, "we're after the diamonds."

"The MAYBE diamonds! which we hadn't gotten close enough to see. Because the light was too dim. Which is why we were waiting. WAITING! For the chance to see. To make sure. Which would have told us that these are not diamonds. Not anything. Just garbage. And now you've scared him off for good. I don't suppose you found him before you grabbed this piece of junk, moron?"

"N-n-no, he wasn't there." He was trying to regain his sense of certainty. "He wasn't coming! So I acted! He wasn't coming!"

"How the fuck do you know that? The same way you knew these were fucking diamonds?" Unable to contain his anger anymore, he tore the non-diamond from the yarmulka and threw it into the other's face. His rage unabated, he followed up with a few smacks across the face with the hat itself.

Realizing he had screwed up, the shorter man decided the best thing for him to do was retreat until the boss had calmed down. He would figure out a way to fix the situation and redeem himself later. He stepped back to get out of the range of the hand smacking him; when it followed, he took a few more steps back raising his hands to cover his face which was being pummeled by fists now. He continued backing up, his hands covering his face against the onslaught, until he tripped over a rusty pipe and crashed to the ground. When he stayed down, the taller man gave him a brutal kick. "Get up!" When this had no effect and the prone body didn't move, he leaned over and felt for the non-existent pulse.

"Shit, stupid fucker." Throwing the yarmulka with its worthless sparkles onto the corpse, he gave the body a final kick and stormed off in disgust.

∞

AFTER A GLORIOUS DAY spent alone at home, Bella went in on Monday afternoon to do the paperwork she hadn't had time for the previous week (too many visitors!). She looked forward to seeing 'her' yarmulka, but as she neared *objets*, what she saw instead was a broken window partially covered by cardboard. *Oh no! maybe this wasn't such a good block to open such a nice store in!* She looked round, but neither of the owners were in sight.

Her brother surprised her by appearing a few hours later. This was unusual enough for her to immediately ask: "What's wrong? Is it Ma?"

"Can't I drop in on my own store from time to time? After all, I am a part owner...," he teased her.

"Well, yes, of course," she stammered, "it's just …."

"I know, it's not something I've ever done before."

"Right," she said, relieved that there was no mother problem. Their mother had fallen a few times in the recent past, obliging Bella and Carl to rearrange their lives to deal with the crises.

"I was in the neighbourhood because of the break-in. You know, the store on the next block?"

"Yes, yes, I saw the broken window. Are they okay? Was anyone hurt?"

"I just took the report – looks like they only smashed the window, broke some stuff and took an old statue and also, of all things, a yarmulka!"

"Oh no!" Bella wailed.

Carl looked surprised, "I thought you'd get a kick out of that."

"It was so beautiful," she explained. "It wasn't an ordinary yarmulka."

"No, I guess not," Carl looked at his notebook, "feathers and crystals. Not like any yarmulka I've ever seen."

"That's all they took?"

"Seems so. Maybe just for fun, it certainly wasn't worth much, not like the old statue, which was a Mayan artifact."

"I suppose…. The yarmulka was really beautiful though, and unique. Did you talk to Zelda and Daniel?"

"Just the woman. Zelda? He wasn't there. She said she hasn't seen him since last week." He hesitated a moment, then added, "By the way, Anna's back from vacation and wants to have a family dinner on Friday. She says we haven't had one in a couple of months, what with people being away."

Bella frowned. "What? She's afraid to ask me herself?"

"Maybe …."

When her scowl deepened, he added, "They're not so bad."

"I suppose. Maybe it's residual reaction from all those years before."

"So can you come?" he persisted. Somehow, in the last few years, he'd ended up closer than her to the rest of their family. None of them had ever been close. But it was Bella, one year older than Carl, who had followed their older sister around until Anna stopped finding it amusing; then, in later years, Anna and Bella had occasionally gotten together for a movie or a drink. In the old days, the only time their entire family got together was for the annual Passover ordeal. Recently, the family had experienced a rapprochement and had shared the occasional Friday night dinner. He, Bella, their mother, and cousin Lila with her husband George and their three daughters, had gathered at Anna's house where her husband Eddie cooked delicious meals for them. Carl had found himself enjoying these dinners and now looked forward to them. Bella didn't share his enthusiasm.

"I guess, yes. But I'll be late, I'm by myself in the store until Raoul gets back. So I have to close up here first."

"Great! I'll let her know. See you on Friday."

Bella had finished the accounts by then, so she went to offer her condolences to Zelda, who was in the window sweeping up broken glass. "I heard about the break-in," Bella commiserated. "I'm so sorry. Usually it's a friendly street. This block has never seemed quite as safe as the one we're on, but nothing like this has happened in all the years I've been here."

"I guess we were just unlucky," Zelda said.

"And they took the yarmulka?"

Zelda nodded. "Along with the Mayan figurine."

"I'm so sorry about the yarmulka – I know you loved it."

Zelda nodded again. "I did. At least they had good taste." They both laughed weakly at her feeble attempt at humour. But Zelda cut her laugh short as she remembered another worry: "Have you seen Daniel? I can't find him anywhere."

"No," said Bella, "not since last week, I'm not sure when."

"He was here Friday, he closed the store, but I haven't heard from him since. He was supposed to open the store this morning, but there's no sign of him. It's not like him to disappear."

"I'm sure he'll show up soon."

"Yes, probably," agreed Zelda, returning to the clearing of debris.

∞

CARL WAS CALLED to the hospital to question a fifteen-year-old boy who, so far, had refused to say anything at all, even his name. He'd been brought in Saturday night, unconscious, with a knife wound that had barely missed his heart. He was now conscious and stable and had been identified by the frantic parents who'd managed to track him down. When Carl entered the hospital room, the boy's eyes flickered open, took in the uniform, and closed immediately.

The woman sitting at his side jumped to her feet. "Finally! You're here to find out who did this terrible thing to my son!"

"Yes, I need to talk to him. To find out what happened."

"You can see what happened! Someone attacked him with a knife. He almost died. He could have died! Where were you when it happened? He could have been killed!"

"Yes, I know," Carl was trying to be diplomatic, "but where? When? I need the details."

They turned to the boy, whose eyes did not open. Together, they watched him in silence. After a few minutes, his mother touched his hand gently. "Sébastien? Are you awake?" When the boy didn't respond, she turned back to Carl. "I'm sorry, he's still asleep."

Although Carl had seen the boy observe his entrance, he knew better than to force the issue. Either the mother was clueless, or else she was protecting her child. Either way, he wasn't likely to get a statement while she was around. His eyes combed the room, searching for anything that might help pinpoint where the boy had been. On the table next to the bed, he found the objects that had been in the boy's pockets. He zeroed in on a peculiar piece of clay. It was just a fragment, but the colouring and markings were striking. Carl had never seen an old Mayan statue, but thought it very possible that a broken-off piece might look like this. Keeping his voice from betraying his excitement, he asked, "What's this?"

"No idea, I've never seen it before. Must be something he picked up somewhere."

"Do you mind if I take it with me?"

She joined him at the table and looked at it more closely. "Why?" she asked. "Is it important?"

"I'm not sure," he responded, "but it might help."

She gestured her consent, already turning back to her immobile son.

Carl's supervisor also thought it looked a lot like a Mayan fragment. And the boy had been found just a couple of blocks from *objets*. They would have to wait for the expert to confirm this, but in the meantime the break-in was given a higher priority and assigned to Detective Stéphane Martin.

∞

ZELDA CONTINUED sweeping up the broken glass.

She'd been collecting these objects for a long time, hoping that she'd one day be able to realize her dream of opening a store. She'd supported herself as a midwife and yoga instructor, and collected the objects lovingly, one by one, as she found them. These had been supplemented by Daniel's choices, which made the assortment even more eclectic. The yarmulka, the centrepiece, had been a recent addition. And then Pedro showed up with his Mayan figurine, which they'd added at the last minute. Although exquisite, it was too small to draw attention to itself, so Daniel had positioned it next to the shiny new teapot, where the contrast made it more eye-catching. It was the most expensive item in the window, in the whole store. And it'd been stolen. With the yarmulka. Besides those two, nothing was missing. A few objects had been injured, but the damage was mostly to the window itself. She brushed the glass shards off Daniel's mask and laid it gently on the table in the store. The medieval wig that she'd carried back so carefully from England was also full of glass splinters, but so numerous and so small that they had embedded themselves into the hair; she would see if it could be salvaged. The fat Buddha, a little dented but otherwise intact, still smiled from an odd angle on the floor. The Barbie executive was looking a little worse for wear, her suit stained and her hair askew.

She kept working, struggling to focus on the task at hand and not think about the stolen yarmulka. She was afraid that if she did, she would start crying again. It was the same attachment that made it impossible for her to think of selling it – she'd infused it with her heart and soul. It was her first yarmulka and still the best one, the most beautiful, the most alluring and attractive. But it was more than that, much more. There was also the inspiration behind it, the attachment to her family, her early life, her mother whom she'd been missing that weekend. She'd left Winnipeg at 18, ecstatically happy to leave the constrained life of family and community. Too many rules and traditions, too many dos and don'ts. She'd hated the small townishness, with everyone knowing her business and not shy about offering their opinions. She'd left as soon as she could, first to a small liberal arts college in Ohio, then on to California. She'd inhaled the freedom she found in these places and created a new life for herself, where she could choose, could set her own path, could be whatever she wanted, could invent and reinvent herself as often as she liked. And, most importantly, there was no one watching and criticizing, or having expectations that had nothing to do with her and her values. It had been so extraordinarily liberating!

She'd discovered Wicca at college, but it wasn't until she'd been in Berkeley for a few years that she found a coven that resonated with her inner being. Her coven-mates became her new family, a community with only one rule, the Wiccan principle of not doing harm to anyone or anything. It was more powerful than karma: in the Wiccan version, whatever good a person did was returned to them three times over; whatever bad they did also came back tripled.

By the time she crocheted the yarmulka, she'd been living in Montreal for two years. She'd moved there with a partner who had since departed, but by then Zelda had fallen in love with the city itself, so she stayed.

She'd visited Winnipeg every once in a while since her departure, but not too often. Her father had died during her California years and she'd made an effort to see her mother a little more often after that. Her mother, more and more confused as she got older, had died the year before and Zelda had found herself missing her. So when her sister invited her to her grandson's Bar Mitzvah, Zelda surprised them both by accepting .

She'd spent the whole weekend feeling the absence of her mother. Her mother had not crocheted, but Zelda imagined she'd have approved of her new skill and when she'd started working on the yarmulka, she'd sensed her mother's presence. In a box of trinkets, she found a cat brooch she'd bought for her mother. She remembered how she'd gone to Woolworth's and how her mother had reacted as if she'd received the crown jewels, and how she'd continued to wear that tacky brooch on special occasions until one of the cheap stones fell out. Zelda carefully removed the remaining stone from the other eye. She cast a spell of love and safety around it, using her most powerful magic, calling on both the Goddess and the God, invoking all the elements. She placed the former cat's eye on her lap and sat in the centre of a pentagram while crocheting. She finished by attaching the glittering stone.

The result was powerful enough for the magic to affect others as well; Bella was the latest but not the only one who'd been drawn in. She'd even had a visit from a Hasidic girl who looked about twelve, who'd come in very shyly and nervously and asked about it. Neither of them had mentioned the word yarmulka and Zelda had no idea if the Ultra-Orthodox Jewish girl realized what it was. She'd offered to make one for the girl, who'd shaken her head and withdrawn quickly after looking around to make sure no one had seen her.

So Zelda wasn't entirely surprised that it had been stolen. Its powerful attractive force was probably just too strong for the thief to resist. She tried to focus on the positive: that s/he who took it was wearing and enjoying it, that this was just a way of spreading joy and happiness throughout the world. But she was having trouble fending off the feeling that her mother had been ripped away from her yet again.

To add to her desolation, Daniel wasn't there to help in this crisis. He'd become such a support all those days they'd worked together to build the store, from its inception as a vision in her mind, to a brick and mortar reality.

He was gone too. Without a word. Which was very worrying. He seemed to have deep secrets that haunted him and, by osmosis, scared her. He'd calmed down a lot from when she first met him, when he'd been so jumpy and anxious. She'd introduced him to Wicca, to the chanting and meditations of her Wiccan practice. They'd spent hours chanting and meditating and she'd seen how it helped him, how he became more tranquil, less nervous. But now he'd vanished. Without a word. She had a feeling it was better not to involve the police. She didn't even know where he was from. He never talked about his past, but she didn't think it was a happy story. She hoped he was off somewhere having such a fun time that he'd forgotten to call. The knot in her gut reminded her how unlike him that would be.

She was trying very hard not to see all this as bad. She didn't like bad. She chanted every day, she lit candles and incense, to keep bad away from her. She tried to do good as often as she could, to help others, so that the good would return to her thrice over. She didn't think she'd done anything to deserve the opposite, and she hoped most fervently that there wasn't a third disaster waiting.… She needed to call her coven together as soon as possible, to undo the negative energy in her store and in her life, and to protect Daniel, wherever he was.

∞

NOEMI RESURFACED ON TUESDAY, sore feet and back firmly in place. Raoul, returned from his vacation, nodded at her from the window. Although not one of his usual workdays, he'd come in at Bella's request to change the display. Noemi hardly noticed him as she limped over to the chair.

"I hope you don't mind," she appealed to Bella, who had brought her a glass of water as soon as she appeared.

"No that's fine, but I may not have time to talk much today."

"That's okay, you don't need to entertain me. I just couldn't stay home, I had to get out, I was going stir crazy and climbing the walls."

"And dodging Nurit?" Bella asked. "Is she still on at you about the circumcision?"

"No, she's disappeared."

"Disappeared? Just like that? Should we be looking for her?"

"I think it's okay. She said she'd be back in a few days, that was the last we saw of her. Avi says she does this from time to time. Goes completely off the radar, doesn't answer her phone or anything. After a few days, she comes back. Avi's trying to stay calm, you know how excitable he is!"

"Doesn't she say where she's been?"

"Apparently not. The first few times, her parents were worried and tried to find her, but they've gotten used to it. Especially now that she's studying in England, she's not around that much."

"How long's she been there?"

"Going on five years now – she's changed her major three times already."

"And you have no idea where she goes or what she does when she goes AWOL?"

Noemi shook her head, "No, none."

"Strange things are going on," Bella exclaimed, "store break-ins, people vanishing!"

"Babies kicking!" Noemi added as she grabbed her belly. Bella looked on in concern – she had no experience with pregnancy or childbirth and no idea what, if anything, was normal.

"It's okay," Noemi reassured her when the spasm passed, "happens every few hours at this point. I choose to think of it as him adding his vote against circumcision. Avi has a fit when I say that."

Bella got busy with store business and, again, didn't notice when Noemi left. She missed her, though, when Pedro sauntered in; she was starting to think she needed someone to run interference. She'd just hung up the phone when she felt someone close behind her; spinning around, she found herself virtually in his arms with his face several inches from hers.

"Bellísima, you make my dreams come true!" he exulted.

She pushed him away. "Pedro, please."

"I came for your answer, Bellísima."

"To what?"

"To dinner. Will you have dinner with me, my Bellísima?"

"Oh, Pedro, thank you so much for asking, but…."

"But you will think about it?"

She needed to change the subject, to derail him: "I'm so sorry about your statue."

She'd succeeded. The smile was replaced by wariness. "What do you mean?"

Uh oh. "Didn't you hear about the break-in?" When he shook his head, she continued, "At Zelda's store."

"And my figurine?"

"I think it was stolen. Along with her beautiful crocheted yarmulka."

Success! She congratulated herself as he left quickly without mentioning dinner again.

∞

"ZELDA! My Mayan statue!"

She nodded as Pedro burst into *objets*. "Yes," she said sadly, "it's gone. I'm so sorry! I know how much it meant to you and your family."

"Yes, yes, of course, so sad. And it was so valuable. But you're insured? I'll get the money for it?"

"I talked to them already, they just need your papers."

"What papers? What do you mean?"

"Something that shows the value. They need to know how much it's worth. Oh, and they also want the provenance."

"What's that?"

"Something showing you're the legitimate owner." She looked at him suddenly. "You do have something?"

He smiled at her reassuringly. "Oh yes. I will bring a letter from my grandmother."

"Is that all you have?"

"What else would you want?"

"A receipt, a bill of sale…."

"But it has been in my family so long…. I will ask my grandmother."

"Did you ever have it assessed?"

"No…."

"Because, for the claim, they want to know how much it was worth."

"Well, we know that. I can tell you its value."

"I think they would like something more than your word."

"I can show them similar figurines, and how much *they* sell for."

"Let's give them that, then, maybe it will do. Bring me what you have as soon as you can, I'll give them to the insurance adjuster."

"Great! I'll bring them tomorrow!"

She watched him leave in his usual super-confident manner. *First the yarmulka missing, then this. I hope there won't be a problem with the figurine too.*

∞

WHEN AVI BURST into the store, Bella was reminded of his near-hysteria the year before when neighbourhood vandalism had been linked to antisemitic attacks.

"Bella, Bella can I talk to you? Do you have a minute?"

She liked Avi but was wary of his projects; he'd wanted to organize anti-antisemitic patrols the year before. "I guess, but I'm pretty busy," she said unenthusiastically.

Avi plowed on, heedless, "It's about Noemi."

Bella was immediately worried. "Is she okay?" she started to ask, but Avi was too fixated to hear.

"She is just being so unreasonable, so totally difficult, and she won't listen to me, she puts her hands over her ears and leaves the room, I don't know what to do, will you talk to her?" Now he stopped and looked at her expectantly.

"About what?" she asked hesitantly, hoping that this had nothing to do with his and Noemi's argument. Her optimism was immediately squashed.

"It's about the circumcision," here he hesitated, "you *do* know what that is?" He knew her Judaism was somewhat deficient. She nodded.

"She doesn't want to do it!" he exploded.

She nodded again, not wanting to tell him that Noemi had also been ranting to her about it.

After a moment, he went on: "It's preposterous! This is a Jewish boy we're having, and that's what Jewish boys do! They get circumcised. It's what they've always done and what they always WILL do. We're Jews. We're having a boy! A Jewish boy! This is the sign of a Jewish boy, it's a requirement of being Jewish!"

He seemed discomfited by her continued silence and continued at a slightly lower pitch. "Don't you agree? You're Jewish, what do you think? Aren't you going to circumcise your son? EVERYONE does it! Even non-Jews do it. It's healthier, it's better for the boy, the doctors all agree, so why does she have to be different? to disagree with everyone?"

Bella ventured a mild opinion: "Maybe there are two sides to this?"

Even this set him off again: "Only for crazy people! I don't know anyone who hasn't been circumcised! She says it's barbaric torture. That's ridiculous! Even doctors do it, there's nothing barbaric about it, it's what civilized people do!"

Bella felt like she had to continue: "It's just…"

But Avi, in his stride now, cut her off: "All Jews do this, not just Orthodox ones. It has nothing to do with what kind of Jew you are, it's for all Jews. It's what makes them Jewish. Don't you have a brother?" When she nodded, he said, "And isn't he circumcised?"

"I don't know," she said quickly, shutting her mind to the image of her brother's private parts.

"I'm sure he is! Even if your family is completely non-observant, I'm positive. Let's call and ask him!"

"No, no that's okay," she said, even more quickly, "you're probably right."

"I AM right. Because it's what we all do. Even in the war, when it was so dangerous, we did it. To carry on. And we DID carry on, we DID survive. We're still Jews. So, of course, we will do it now, when it isn't dangerous. My parents are coming just to be there, they want to celebrate with us. They would never even begin to understand how there could be a question about it!"

When Bella offered nothing but silence in response, Avi deflated. "Will you speak to her?" he asked plaintively. "Try to make her see sense?"

"I don't think…."

"Please? I don't know what else to do! Please, could you just talk to her about it? Maybe she'll listen to you."

"Avi, I really don't think I'm the right person …."

"You're the only person I can ask, please, I'm begging you. For the sake of our baby, please!"

He wore her down; by the time he left, she'd promised to think about it.

She felt trapped. She didn't like arguments in general, tried to stay away from them, especially from the middle! But she also liked to keep her promises. She tried to persuade herself that this one didn't count, as it'd been made under duress.

By the end of the day, she was tired and grumpy. The walk home didn't help. The display window at *objets* was almost back to its former beautiful enticing splendour, but all Bella could see was the absence of the yarmulka.

∞

ONCE THEY'D ALL ARRIVED, Zelda led her coven-mates into the room where they would perform the ritual. She'd prepared the altar in advance. On the small low table in the centre of the room, she'd placed a bowl of salt, a stick of incense, a candle, a bowl of water, a small bell, and a ceramic goblet decorated with five-pointed pentacles. She'd searched in vain for a photo of Daniel to place on the altar, had had to settle for one of his carved bird masks instead.

Without Daniel, they only had twelve members, not the optimal thirteen. They arranged themselves in a circle, with four of them taking up positions at each of the cardinal points. In her California coven, the high priestess had always been the one to cast the circle, but in the more egalitarian Montreal group, they took turns. As she'd been the one to convene, Zelda performed this sacred activity. As she stepped into the middle of the circle, the others closed their eyes, and all together, they invited the Goddess and God to join them. After a moment of silence, she stepped to the table and lit the incense and candle, poured water and then salt into the goblet, and waved her sacred knife over them, invoking the spirits. Walking outside the circle in a clockwise direction, she stopped at each cardinal point to light a candle and call on the spirits of Air, Fire, Water, and Earth.

Zelda then spoke about Daniel and her fears for his safety. With her knife, she drew a pentagram in the air above the mask that he had carved and recited the protection spell:

> *With this pentagram I do lay*
> *Protection here both night and day.*
> *In the shadows, evils hide,*
> *Ready to draw him from love's side,*
> *But with your help he shall be strong,*
> *Banish all that do him wrong.*
>
> *Send them away, send them astray*
> *Never again to pass his way.*
> *I now invoke the Law of Three:*
> *This is my will, so mote it be!*
> *so mote it be, so mote it be!*

When she'd finished, the coven repeated the spell in unison.

They joined hands again and the priest next to Zelda performed the uncasting of the circle, doing everything she had done in the reverse order and opposite direction. When he'd finished, they filed out of the room as silently as they'd entered.

∞

BACK AT WORK at the local library, Mathieu was finding it hard to interest himself in the stack of paperwork that had accumulated during his absence. He managed to make it through the emails but every time he so much as glanced in the direction of his physical inbox, his eyes started to close and his brain to drift. So he chatted with his coworkers, checked out the New Arrivals, and drank many cups of coffee.

When he still found himself falling asleep midway through the afternoon, he gave up. The fresh air, hot as it was, revived him, and he strolled down the street, enjoying the sounds, smells and sights of summer in the city. He checked out the display window in Belles Fleurs: *Not too shabby.* Ever since Raoul had taken over from Bella, the displays had markedly improved. Raoul combined artistic talent with a quirky, contemporary perspective that matched Mathieu's own tastes.

The theme was a fireworks display, coinciding with the city's International Fireworks Competition. Although imbued with the same minimalist sensibility that Raoul brought to all his creations, it nevertheless managed to suggest the loud explosions of sound that would accompany the bursts of coloured light.

When he got inside, Raoul was at the desk hanging up the phone. Mathieu high-fived him, "Great window again!"

"Thanks! I think you're my biggest fan," was the pleased response.

"Doesn't Bella like them yet?" Raoul had been doing the displays for over a year.

"She doesn't mind, but I'm not sure she actually likes them...."

"I like them!" Bella had heard this as she came in from the back room. When they both immediately raised their eyebrows, she defended her statement: "Well I do like them. I just don't love them."

"I guess that's right. Anyhow, as long as you let me keep doing them...."

"I *want* you to keep on. You're much better at it than me."

Mollified, Raoul went back to putting together the flowers for the order he'd just taken.

"Do you want to go get something to eat?" asked Mathieu turning to Bella. "It's so nice out, we could sit on a *terrasse*, drink a cold beer…."

"I guess I could." Tempted, Bella looked at her watch. "It's past three already, and Raoul is staying for the rest of the day. Okay!"

They were not the only ones lured out by the heat, sun, slight breeze, and cold beer combination. Almost all the local eateries had added outdoor *terrasses*, which ranged from two or three tables placed casually on the sidewalk to more elaborate and permanent constructions. Mathieu and Bella made it to their favourite café in time to grab the last table.

While they waited for their beer, they caught up with each other. They'd become close friends over the eleven years they'd been neighbours. Mathieu, in particular, liked to know details about his friends and neighbours. Bella had gotten used to his nosiness and even come to see its benefit, as it made the neighbourhood safer. She was the opposite, usually didn't ask a single question that could be interpreted as prying. But over the years, she'd begun to ask Mathieu personal questions in return, realizing that he welcomed it as a sign of their friendship.

"How was your time with Nurit?" she asked. "Noemi was so glad you went off with her."

"Why? Doesn't she like her?"

"I think she's too tired to be sociable right now." Bella thought it was okay to bring up the tiredness since Noemi herself mentioned it to everyone she talked to. Anything more seemed like gossip, so she kept quiet about the circumcision conflict.

"I had a great time. And I thought she did too. We really seemed to click, to like the same things, I even thought we might have a future...." A self-conscious wince accompanied this confession, even as he tried to make it sound like a joke. "But then, all of a sudden, she said she had to go and pouf, just like that, no more Nurit. I haven't heard from her since, she hasn't answered my messages."

"Well, if it makes you feel any better, she's disappeared totally."

"What do you mean?"

"Noemi said she does this periodically, just takes off, no one knows where, doesn't answer phone or anything, and then comes back after a while."

Mathieu didn't know if this made him feel better or not. On the one hand, it wasn't just him she was avoiding, but on the other hand, it was also him she was avoiding.

Now Bella was sorry she'd brought up the subject; she knew Mathieu would like a romantic relationship. To distract him, she started telling him about the break-in and other neighbourhood events he'd missed.

"That reminds me!" he exclaimed. "I thought I saw some drug dealing going on the other night. In fact, it was right around that new store. Do you think they might be moving back in?" he asked worriedly. Bella had also been involved in the drug cleanup, and he knew she'd share his concern about the dealers resurfacing. She hadn't seen or heard anything herself, but assured him she'd be on the lookout and spread the word.

They went on to discuss the books each was currently reading, their favourite topic. Although they had radically different tastes, each had learned to appreciate the other's choices and now even sometimes read the other's recommendations.

They sat on the *terrasse* until the sun set, enjoying the summer evening, local beer, and each other's company.

∞

MATHIEU CAME HOME on Thursday to find a message from Nurit on his voicemail. When he called her back, making an effort not to sound too eager, he was pleased to hear enthusiasm in her voice.

"Where've you been?" he asked in the most neutral tone he could manage.

"Nowhere special. Does your offer still stand to continue our tour? I thought it would be fun to hang out here for a couple of weeks but my brother's at work all day, my sister-in-law is super pregnant cranky, and I'm totally bored!"

Obviously she wasn't about to explain anything. Still, she had called and wanted to get together. Determined to focus on the positive, he strove to project a laidback attitude. Hesitating slightly, he said, "I have to work all day," but then added hurriedly before she could think he wasn't interested, "How about tomorrow night?"

"I guess," she sounded less than pleased. "Can't you take the day off?"

He considered it seriously for a moment until he remembered what his very full schedule looked like.

"Sorry," he said regretfully, "I really can't."

He went on quickly, before she could decide she had better options, "There's lots of stuff to do tomorrow night, Friday in the city!" He started listing them: "Festivals downtown, cafes, clubs or even a comic convention...." He slipped in the last option to see if she might possibly be interested.

He usually attended Comiccon, it was always a lot of fun. Not a cos-player himself, he enjoyed the costumes that appeared each year. A while back, he'd been captivated by the Spidermen who climbed walls and swooped down from ceilings. Last year there'd been too many of these, but he'd been delighted by the woman dressed as the USS Enterprise starship and the man who'd shown up as Wonder

Woman. That last memory made him imagine Nurit in a Wonder Woman costume!

He was about to repeat his last suggestion with a bit more enthusiasm, when she broke in with, "Sure, whatever! You decide. See you tomorrow," and got off the phone.

She didn't even notice the comic reference.... A little disappointed, he rebuked himself: *What are you thinking? That all of a sudden life will get perfect? That you'll find a woman you like, who likes you, AND likes comics?*

He turned to Fritz, who opened an eye. "I know, I know. Life is about choices.... I guess I can miss Comiccon this year. Who knows, maybe next year she'll come with me! Maybe even as Wonder Woman...." With that picture filling his mental screen, he dropped down on the couch, forgetful of the cat who had to scramble out of the way to avoid being crushed.

The displaced cat meowed loudly, voicing his displeasure at this lack of respect. Mathieu gathered him onto his lap and scratched in all Fritz's favourite places, while he continued with his fantasy: "Maybe my love life has just taken a turn for the better!" He looked down at the cat who had switched into purring mode. "I'll let you know tomorrow...."

Just in case he might be able to have it all, he suggested the comic convention again the next day, but Nurit's response was extremely tepid. Instead, he took her to a bilingual comedy show. He laughed himself silly, with the rest of the audience, and she enjoyed the jokes she got. They were still laughing as they continued the evening, first in Mathieu's living room and then in his bedroom. He didn't get to see her as Wonder Woman, but the view without any clothes suited him just fine.

∞

RUNNING THE STORE by herself was an inconvenience, to say the least. She'd depended on Daniel to share the day to day stuff, especially the actual presence in the store. If he didn't come back, she was going to have to either hire someone, which she couldn't afford until she started making money, or cut down on the hours, which would also cut down on revenue. Daniel had been willing to work for subsistence wages with the promise of sharing the eventual profits; she wasn't sure anyone else would do that. In the meantime, she was stuck with being in the store as much as she could.

She'd salvaged most of the objects from the window display although, sadly, not her medieval wig. She'd done her best to remove the glass splinters, but the hair had become so tangled around them that it was impossible. She couldn't bring herself to throw it out, though, and harboured the hope that she might be able to incorporate some of it into something else. Maybe something crocheted? She planted that seed in the back of her brain for future consideration, she'd found from experience that some of her most creative efforts were a result of those ruminations.

She'd cleaned up Barbie, who once again looked ready to take on her Board. The window had been replaced and there was no more evidence of the break-in, other than the lost yarmulka, visible only in her heart. And Pedro's lost figurine which, at least for her, held no sentimental value.

Now she was inside the store, enjoying the soft lighting, soothing music and lovely objects she was surrounded by. Trying to make her time productive, she picked up the yarmulka she was currently working on. *I'd better work a little faster, at least I can get paid for this.*

She'd almost finished the crocheting part when the phone rang. She pounced on it eagerly, hoping the spell had worked and that Daniel was back. But it was the police, calling to inform her that her stolen yarmulka had been found. This was also welcome news.

"That's terrific," she exclaimed, "when can I have it back?"

"Not soon, I'm afraid. First of all, you should know that it's been damaged."

Uh oh, she felt that as a punch to her gut. "How badly?"

"It's torn and dirty and seems to have had some of the ornaments ripped off."

Maybe not a total disaster? "I can probably repair it."

"The problem is, it was found with a person. A body."

It took her a moment to comprehend what he'd said. "A body? As in a dead body?"

"Yes, I'm afraid so. We need to keep your hat as evidence."

This was making less and less sense. "Evidence? Of what? You mean someone was killed?"

"We think so, maybe. We're waiting for the results of the autopsy, but we think this person may have been the victim of foul play. So we need to hold on to the hat. But we want to know if you can identify both the hat and the victim."

Oh no! Please, dear Goddess, please don't let it be Daniel! "Do you know who it is? He? Or she?"

"It's a man, a black man, but no, we don't know who he is. That's why we'd like to show you a picture and see if you can identify him."

Inspector Martin had decided not to mention the clay fragment for a number of reasons. First, he hadn't completely ruled her out as a suspect. She'd sounded dumbfounded on the phone, but he'd brought his partner along, just in case, to take note of her expression when she saw the picture of the dead man. Plus there was the possibility that it wasn't related to her valuable and maybe irreplaceable stolen statue after all, as this hadn't yet been confirmed by the expert. He also hadn't talked to the boy himself, so he had no idea how it connected with the robbery or the dead man in the empty warehouse. Whereas the knitted hat-thing had been found with the dead body. Better to stick with what they knew for now. That would probably upset her enough; he didn't want a hysterical woman on his hands if he could avoid it. And she certainly seemed nervous when they entered the store, although that was not surprising, given the circumstances.

Zelda had, in fact, been completely agitated since the phone call, so worried about Daniel she couldn't think of anything else. That worry was momentarily forgotten when she saw her beautiful yarmulka. Even torn and dirty, enclosed in an evidence bag, she still felt its pull and her tears welled up. She reached for it eagerly. The taller detective's arm stopped her and his words reawakened her anxiety. It was part of an investigation into a suspicious death. They hadn't finished the forensic analysis. She couldn't touch it yet.

They did allow her to hold the bag when they realized how distressed she was and saw her tears. She tried to control these so she could focus on the picture the other man was holding out to her. The fear that it was Daniel was so overwhelming that it was a struggle to stay upright. When he pulled back, her vision cleared for a moment, and she realized she didn't know the man in the picture.

"No, no, sorry," she shook her head, joyful, "I have no idea who he is."

The Inspector was a little suspicious of her reaction, but he hadn't had much hope that she would recognize the dead man. It seemed more likely that the statue was the target, and her shop and hat were incidental. He'd read the initial report, but took her through the details again. "Where did you get the statue from?"

"It's not actually mine. We have it on consignment."

"Is it valuable?"

"A little, it's a couple of hundred years old."

He checked his notes. "Not an ancient artifact?"

"Well, that depends on what you mean by ancient. It's more like a modern artifact. Made by Mayans, but not the ancient ones."

"Who is the owner?" Maybe the dead man had been tracking the statue, from when it was still in the hands of the owner. In which case the owner might recognize him.

"Pedro … sorry, I can't remember his last name. I have his phone number, if you want it."

When he nodded, she went into the back room. He followed her, more from habit than because he thought she'd make a run for it or pull a gun. Sure enough, all she did was open a filing cabinet, from which she retrieved Pedro's co-ordinates.

As they turned to go, she asked hopefully, "Do you know when I can have my yarmulka back?"

"No, sorry, we'll let you know."

"Well?" he asked as they got back in the car. "Do you think she was lying?"

His partner shook his head. "Didn't look it to me."

"Me neither. Oh well, back to the databases."

"She sure seemed attached to that hat thing, though!"

"Yeah, who'd have thought. Good thing we didn't tell her about the statue being broken!"

∞

ZELDA WALKED BY as Bella was locking the front door, and stopped to tell her the news: "They found my yarmulka!"

"Oh that's wonderful."

"Yes, it is, but I can't have it back yet because it's evidence." At Bella's inquiring look, she explained, "It's very strange, they found it with a dead man. One I've never seen before. They're calling it a suspicious death."

"What does that mean?"

"I don't know. And I really don't know what it has to do with my yarmulka!"

"Has Daniel turned up yet?"

"No. We did a protection ritual for him. My coven," she added at Bella's puzzled look. "But no word. I'm so worried."

"Hopefully he's off somewhere having too good a time to get in touch?" Bella proposed this platitude, feeling she had to say something reassuring. "Did you ask the police to look for him?"

"No! No, I can't do that."

"Why not?"

"I... I think he might have been in some kind of trouble before. He's always so nervous, especially around the police. I'm sorry, I shouldn't have said anything. Please don't mention this to anyone, don't tell anyone he's gone, or what I just said. In fact, please just forget I said anything!"

Zelda was so distraught that Bella assured her it was long forgotten and that she would never mention it to a soul. Then, remembering that she was already late for the family Friday night dinner, she hurriedly said goodbye and ran to catch her bus. She squeezed herself on and tried not to grab onto the body in front of her as the bus raced through the orange light. Even with all this jerking about, part of her mind was thinking about Zelda's news. *So very strange. Break-ins are rare enough in this neighbourhood, but suspicious deaths? And disappearances? Shady pasts? Not welcome news at all.*

∞

CARL SAT AT the dining room table, a small part of his attention focused on his mother (this had become automatic since her brief hospitalization the year before), but most of his mind was elsewhere, on the disturbing emotions inside him. He felt like it must be obvious to everyone around him, but nobody seemed to have noticed. Lila's three rambunctious daughters continued their rampaging while their parents looked on helplessly; his mother chattered to Anna, who was in her usual defensive eyes-open sleep posture; Eddie was just bringing food in from the kitchen, trying to avoid bumping into any of the girls as they raced around the room. None of them seemed to notice anything out of the ordinary. They were used to him being quiet.

He felt far removed from his normal equilibrium. He'd received a letter from Jake the day before and had still not recovered his balance. Jake, his former live-in partner, was in jail and had been for the last couple of years. He'd been blindsided by the discovery that neither of them had really known the other at all, and then he'd arrested and brought him in. At which point, Carl had assumed their relationship was over and had closed off that part of himself. Now Jake had written to say that he'd like to communicate with him, that he wanted forgiveness.

Nothing showed on his blank face; Carl tried to keep his feelings from ever showing. It was a habit he'd picked up very young, growing up in a household where there were too many emotions flying around: his over-the-top mother constantly arguing with his almost-as-bad father, until the latter had had enough and left them all, never to return. Then his excitable grandfather joined them on a permanent basis. Carl had learned to make himself as invisible as possible and had never shed the cloak.

Inside was another matter entirely and, until he'd met Jake, it was a private space no one had ever entered. But somehow Jake had penetrated his armour. For the first time, he'd found it possible to face another human being without layers of protection. Because he'd thought that

Jake really saw him, really understood him, really recognized and grasped his most inner self. And, similarly, he'd thought that he really knew Jake. But that turned out not to be the case. Not only had Jake committed a heinous crime, he had done so for both their sakes, thinking that Carl would want him to. Which showed how little they really knew of each other. How could he have been so wrong? How could he have opened himself to someone like that? His exposed heart had cracked. He hadn't regathered the broken pieces. Instead, he'd reconstructed the outer armour and gotten on with his life, on an even keel if not happy. Carl liked even keels.

Now his balance was being threatened all over again. Jake's note had awakened feelings of desire and anger, which flowed through him in alternating waves.

> Hello Carl
> I realize how wrong I was. I am very sorry for the pain I caused you and I hope you can forgive me.
> Hoping to hear from you,
> Jake.

So here he sat, trying to absorb the fact that Jake had been in touch, trying to understand his own reaction, trying to figure out what his reaction even was! He felt as if he were being torn apart by all the conflicting feelings. None of this showed on the face he presented to his family as he sat there, eating and nodding to his mother periodically.

IT WAS A NEW SENSATION for Bella to arrive late for a family affair, one she found very agreeable as she got to her sister's house and saw the rest of them already assembled at the dinner table. *I need to practice this. Coming late means a shorter evening!* Even if the dinners over the last year had ranged from not-awful to even-some-enjoyable-moments, years of dreading any get-together with her family was a habit not easily disregarded.

"Sorry, we couldn't wait for you," Anna apologized, "but you know how it is with kids," pointing to the three girls, who were eating with gusto. As soon as she saw Bella, Yolly, the eldest, put down her fork, jumped up, and ran towards her.

"I've been waiting for you!" she cried out.

Uh oh, what now? Yolly had a tendency to launch herself with great exuberance into whatever project caught her fancy.

"Let her sit down," Lila said in a feeble voice, which her daughter ignored. Bella echoed her cousin's suggestion, saying, "Can I at least sit down first?", forcing Yolly to modify her strategy of direct assault. Not so easily put off, she plunked herself back on her chair and patted the empty one next to her.

"Here!" she barked, "Here's your seat. Come. Sit." Lila shrugged, helpless in the face of her daughter's determination. Bella obediently slid into the chair Yolly indicated, but managed to introduce her own needs into the agenda:

"Mmm," she inhaled the aromas, "smells delicious. What did Eddie make this time?" The reformed alcoholic, who had turned into an excellent cook, smiled at her, acknowledging the newly-friendly relationship between them, as he brought in her plate.

"It may be a little cold," he apologized, "I didn't want it to dry out in the oven."

"I'm sure it's perfect," she responded. "It smells heavenly and I'm starved!" She lifted up a forkful of mushroom risotto and, not looking in the direction of the young cousin sitting next to her watching every move intently, put it into her mouth.

Yolly had grown marginally more patient, or else her parents had succeeded in teaching her a modicum of manners, because she actually waited for Bella to swallow the mouthful before she pounced. But just barely: she watched Bella's throat and as soon as she saw the food go down, the words leaped out of her mouth.

"Tell me about the murder!"

Surprised into responding right away, Bella turned to Yolly: "How do you know about that? I just heard about it. And what do you mean murder? I only heard suspicious death!"

"I've been listening to the police radio!" she smirked.

This assertion of Yolly's got Carl's full attention. His head snapped around towards her at the same time Lila let out a horrified gasp, after which Yolly hurriedly added, "No, no, just kidding. It was on the news."

"You watch the news?" Bella asked, incredulous.

"On Google, you know, Google News! Gotta keep up with what's happening. You never know when a detective's skills will be called for."

Yolly was obsessed with the idea of being a detective. She'd progressed from Nancy Drew to Sherlock Holmes, and was currently reading her way through the books and watching the original film versions as well as numerous modern adaptations. Lila had just barely talked her out of walking around with a pipe in her mouth; she was still trying to convince her parents to buy her a deerstalker hat like Sherlock's.

"Are there any clues?" she now asked eagerly. At Bella's shrug and head shake, she turned expectantly to Carl, who had continued to pay attention. He also shrugged.

"A break-in. They took an old statue. Oh yes, and, of all things, a yarmulka." Carl added this last piece, thinking the rest of his family might find it more amusing than Bella had.

"But it was so beautiful." Bella felt obliged to defend it.

Yolly instantly picked up on this as a source of information: "Did you see it? Do you know the man who died?"

Bella couldn't help laughing at her relentlessness: "Yes I saw the yarmulka and no, I didn't see the man." She stopped with that, remembering Zelda's insistence that she not mention Daniel.

Any contact at all with a 'case' was enough for Yolly: "Can I come look for clues? Please please please Auntie Bella!! I'm off school now, I can even come on my own."

This was too much for her mother, who interrupted anxiously: "No absolutely not, you can NOT go downtown on your own."

Even while Bella was trying to correct her cousin's erroneous idea of where she lived with a "It's not downtown," she was drowned out by Yolly's loud protest: "Why not? I'm 11 already."

The skirmish caught her sisters' attention. Nine-year-old Molly and seven-and-a-half-year-old Polly usually rolled their eyes and stayed away from their sister's enthusiasms, but loud conflict with their mother promised excitement. Molly chimed in with a "I wanna go too," echoed by Polly's "Me too! Me too!"

Lila sighed, exasperated with her eldest daughter: "See what you started!"

"But I'm older. I'm not even at daycamp anymore like they are. I'm old enough. Really I am." She'd turned on her most reasonable voice, trying to sound like a mature and responsible adult who could travel by herself. She came up with another argument she could use and turned to Bella, still trying to sound controlled and adult-like: "I could help you at the store. Isn't your assistant away on vacation? Don't you need help?"

Realizing Carl must have told them her reason for being late, Bella couldn't help but admire Yolly's ingenuity. She would definitely be a force to be reckoned with it if she ever put all that brainpower to a productive use! She started to explain that Raoul was back now but her explanation got lost in Yolly's deluge. Like a predator alert to every nuance of her prey's behaviour, Yolly had sensed a possible victory and pressed her advantage. She'd always been stubborn. Ever since Carl had taken her for a ride in his patrol car last year during another of her 'cases,' she'd become unstoppable.

"Please please, Auntie Bella, please. I'll be so much help, you'll see, you'll be so glad to have me there." Bella looked around for help. But Lila had never been able to withstand any of her children and George was little better. They both looked ready to say yes, just to appease their eldest. She looked at Carl, who kept his face neutral. Yolly had left him alone after he told her he couldn't repeat the patrol car ride because regulations forbade it; he'd had to get a special dispensation for the one ride. Bella had no such excuse.

"How would you get there?" She hoped that Lila or George would forbid it. But Yolly had figured everything out: "If they (pointing at her parents) take me to the metro, you could meet me at the other end. I can take the metro by myself," she glared fiercely at her parents, daring them to disagree, "I *am* 11 after all."

Her suburban parents, who did not venture into the city very often or onto public transportation ever, tried to argue that it wasn't safe. But Yolly had an answer ready for that as well.

"I'll take my cell phone," she said. "We can talk the whole time so you'll know I'm okay."

∞

BELLA WALKED SLOWLY to work the next morning, still be-
mused by her little cousin. Part of her had to smile in admiration at the way she'd managed everything to her satis-
faction, while another part cringed at the image of Yolly
joining her at work. The arrangements had been made for
Tuesday when, it was true, she was alone in the store, as
Raoul worked Thursday to Saturday. Lila would drive Yolly
to the first metro station on the line, then call Bella to tell
her Yolly was starting off. Lila and Yolly would then estab-
lish cell phone contact, which they would continue until
Yolly was safely in the hands of a responsible adult, i.e.
Bella. Carl had been able to assure them that the metro had
recently installed cell phone access on this line, so their
plan sounded feasible.

Passing *objets*, she looked in the window as usual and,
as usual, noticed the absence of her yarmulka. Even though
it was not there, she felt its attractive force. What was it
about that yarmulka that so enchanted her? And the fact
that it was somehow tied to a suspicious death, or maybe
even a murder, what was that about? Was something sinis-
ter going on? Something connected to witchcraft? She tried
to shrug off this ridiculous notion, but it refused to dis-
solve.

∞

"ZELDA! Are you here? ZELDA!"

She came running from the back room. She'd become
uncharacteristically panicky, between worrying about Daniel and the break-in, dead bodies and stolen yarmulkas.
When she saw it was Pedro, she stopped to catch her
breath. "What is it? What's the matter?"

"I brought you the papers. For the insurance. So you
can go ahead with the claim."

She leafed through the printouts from eBay showing
various Mayan figurines with their asking prices.

"What about the provenance?"

"The what?"

"You remember – we talked about this yesterday. You said you could get a letter from your grandmother about how it came into your possession?"

"Oh, right…she is very slow, my *abuela*. I will ask her to hurry. But you will go ahead with the claim now?"

"I think we need the letter first – that's what they said when I talked to them."

"Okay, I will try to hurry her. But maybe you could send these other papers in to get them started?"

"Maybe, but try to get the letter."

As Pedro's smile wilted slightly, she remembered the detectives' visit. "Did the police get hold of you?"

He stiffened. "Police?"

"The ones investigating the break-in. They showed me a picture yesterday, they wanted to show it to you too."

"Did you give them my number?"

"Yes, of course I did." She peered at him more closely. "What's wrong? Didn't they call you?"

"Maybe they tried to get in touch. My phone died on me, I forgot to charge it. And I'll be out and about all day today so I won't know if they call…. Maybe you could take care of it for me."

"How could I do that? I have no idea if you would recognize the guy."

"Oh, right, I guess, of course. I know! Maybe you could get a copy of the picture then I'll come by and take a look."

∞

SATURDAY MORNING, Mathieu got out of bed reluctantly, when the scratching on the bedroom door got too persistent to ignore. He arrived in the kitchen just in time to save the wine glasses from being catapulted off the counter by an agitated cat.

"Stop it Fritz! I'm here now." He stooped to smooth the angry cat's fur and scratch the usually-favoured spot behind the left ear. Fritz ignored his conciliatory overtures and stomped over to the back door, looking back expectantly.

"Okay, okay." Mathieu opened the door and the cat ran outside. "I get that you don't like being banished from my bed," he called after the departing back, "but you weren't very nice last night, were you?"

"What was that about?" Nurit asked as he crawled back into bed.

"Just an unhappy cat."

It was obvious that she was not a cat person. She'd looked from him to Fritz when he introduced them, seeming to find Mathieu peculiar for bothering with such childishness. She'd said hello, but then forgotten the cat's existence. Fritz, for his part, had turned around and stalked off. Not an auspicious beginning.

He and Nurit spent most of Saturday and Sunday in bed, surfacing only for food and other necessities. Fritz did not reappear until she vacated the premises.

Week 5

By the time he started high school, the city had changed completely. Ravaged during the civil war because it was a stronghold of the rebels, the city had now rediscovered and recreated itself as a centre of oil production. He'd worked hard at school, dedicating himself to his studies. It paid off when his good grades and polite demeanour got him into the brand new high school built for the privileged children of oil workers and foreigners, rather than the ramshackle overcrowded one for everyone else.

The neighbour who had taken him in was kind, she had also taken in the orphaned babies from across the street; hers was the only family in their neighbourhood not decimated by the lengthy violence. All around them, elderly grandmothers and young children brought up the newly-formed families cobbled together from those who had survived.

She was kind, but her children were not. They had never been happy about the overcrowding in their own house and now they allied themselves with the neighbourhood children who resented his good fortune. He had no luck making friends at his new school either, where he was ignored and excluded. His only friend was his little brother, who continued to prefer his company to any other. Fernando was his opposite: sweet, friendly, he drew people to him. Nando stuck steadfastly by his side, and the two of them spent much time together, enjoying each other's company, despite the ten years difference between them.

∞

MATHIEU HAD DRAGGED himself out of bed on Monday morning, resenting the fact that he had to go to work. He rushed off, regretful and a little sore. He didn't remember Fritz until he'd gotten to the library. Assailed by guilt, he left a message on Bella's voicemail, asking her to keep a lookout for him. *I'll make it up to him. He'll just have to get over it. And maybe, hopefully, he'll have to get used to it!* Mathieu knew

he himself would have no trouble adapting. In the meantime, the lack of sleep and the unaccustomed sexual
workout had put him into a semi-fog, yawning and fantasizing his way through the day.

He cut through the park on his way home, hoping that
the fresh air would revive him. But it was smoke that he
inhaled instead, and as he raised his head, he saw it ema-
nating from a group of teenagers clustered around a bench
talking to someone. When they saw him coming, the teenagers took off on their bikes. Mathieu reached the woman,
now sitting alone and smoking.

"Hi, I haven't seen you here before," he said in a neutral
voice.

"No," was the reply, "you haven't."

Mathieu liked to know what was going on in his community; he thought of himself as its guardian, making the
area that much safer.

"Do you live around here?"

Her voice frosted over. "Why do you want to know?"

"If you live here, I'd welcome you to our neighbourhood!" Mathieu was good at sounding friendly rather than
nosy.

"Oh, well, that's nice of you. I don't live around here,
but I have a friend who does. Maybe you know her? Bella?
She has a flower store."

"Oh, yes, of course I know her. You're a friend of
Bella's?"

"An old friend – we went to high school together." She
stuck out her hand to grasp his: "Emkay."

"Mathieu," he responded. "Pleased to meet you."

"Likewise!"

He remembered the teenagers surrounding her bench.
"Were those kids bothering you just now?"

"Oh no," she laughed, "they were just being kids. They
wanted to bum a cigarette."

"You didn't give them one?"

"Sure I did. Why not?"

"You shouldn't do that!"

She shrugged off his disapproval. Her look of disdain made him feel like he was from a different generation, despite their similar age.

∞

BELLA HAD FORGOTTEN that Yolly was coming. She was still at home when Lila phoned and barely managed to get to the rendezvous point on time. After that, her cousin's retrieval went flawlessly. Yolly burst out of the metro station, wide-eyed and a little subdued. Bella did a double take when she saw the pipe in the 11-year-old's mouth, until she realized it was made of licorice. Yolly handed her phone to Bella, who assured the still-on-line Lila that her daughter had made it safely and looked completely unharmed by the experience. A relieved-sounding mother finally hung up after reminding them of the reverse procedure for the homeward journey. They were left to their day.

Bella wasn't sure what to do with her cousin, but she needn't have worried. First of all, Yolly wasn't used to being in the city, she didn't get there often and had never been without her parents, so she was a little more restrained than usual. She was very aware that this was a trial and that a successful outcome could set a precedent for other, many other, such outings. So she was on her best behaviour. She stayed close to Bella, listening carefully to everything she said.

This was Yolly's first time in Belles Fleurs. She stood in open-mouthed admiration of the window while Bella unlocked the door. "Nice," she commented as she tamely followed Bella inside. "What would you like me to do first?"

Bella had to laugh at her eagerness to work. "Well, why don't you have a look around while I do the opening up," she suggested. As she went through her morning routine, carefully avoiding singing and spinning, she was aware of Yolly exploring the little store, checking out the plants, the flowers, the display window from the inside, even the back room. "What do you think?" Bella asked when they sat down.

"Nice, I guess, the flowers are pretty. It's kind of small, isn't it?"

Yolly trying to be tactful was a new experience for Bella. Not wanting to discourage this previously-unseen side of her cousin, Bella kept her face neutral, "Well, yes, it's not very big. But lots of stores are this size around here. Are your stores bigger?"

"Yes!" Yolly started in a bellow, then toned it back down to her best-behaviour level, "Yes, they are."

Bella nodded, "That's one of the differences between the inner city and the suburbs."

"That's okay," Yolly said magnanimously, "I'm sure they have other compensating factors."

Bella managed to keep her amusement from showing. "You'll tell me at the end of the day if you think this one has any."

She got Yolly opening boxes and unloading supplies, then stowing these carefully into the limited space. *It's true*, she realized, *the store is small*. She shuddered at the idea of being in the suburbs, much in the same way that Lila had flinched at the picture of her daughter venturing into the city.

The morning went well and lunch was a huge success. When the bakery next door offered a choice of freshly-baked croissants or bagels for their sandwiches, Yolly was thrilled. Apparently, this was one city-treat not readily available in her part of the world. Bella smiled smugly.

Noemi came by after they'd finished eating. "Sorry to keep bugging you; I really hope you don't mind?" she beseeched Bella. "I needed to walk because I had some pains this morning." At Bella's gasp of concern, she hurriedly added: "False labour, apparently not unusual in the last month." Bella assured her she could hang out there as much as she wanted, then added worriedly, "But I don't know anything about pregnancy. You'll let me know if there's anything I should be doing?"

Noemi shrugged. "It's just a matter of waiting now."

As Bella went to get her something to drink, Yolly appeared at the back door, towing the recycling container she'd just emptied into the outside bin. When she saw Noemi, she stopped short and stared at the protruding belly which Noemi's skin-tight dress displayed in detail.

"Oh!" she blurted out, at which Noemi's eyes flew open. The two of them stared at each other for a moment, then Noemi said, "Hi, I'm Noemi," at the same time that Yolly said, "You're very pregnant!" They both laughed at that, and Noemi conceded the point: "Yes, I am."

Bella came back with the juice and introduced them: "Noemi, my cousin Yolly."

"Yes, we got there," said Noemi. "Yolly was just telling me I was pregnant."

"Don't they have that where you live?" Bella teased her cousin; but Yolly responded seriously, "Yes but they don't wear such tight dresses!"

Worried that Noemi might be offended by Yolly's tactlessness, Bella started to apologize and stopped when she saw that Noemi was laughing, looking more cheerful than when she'd first come in. After drinking some of the juice, she returned to her more miserable state.

"If anything, it's getting worse at home. Avi got totally freaked out by the pains, and even more insistent about the circumcision. Because now it will be soon. And his parents will be here soon. And Nurit is back and is as bad as him. What is it with those two? They are grownups and so afraid of their parents!"

Bella became aware of her cousin, listening intently. She didn't know if this was a 'child appropriate' conversation, but concluded that Yolly was not exactly delicate or in need of sheltering. Yolly had indeed zeroed in on the mention of circumcision, but not for the male-body-part aspect. She was drawn by what it revealed about Noemi.

"You're Jewish?" she asked in an amazed voice.

When Noemi confirmed this, saying, "Yes, from Morocco," Yolly got so excited she started jumping up and down, exclaiming, "Me too! My dad's Moroccan! My real name is Yolande!"

Having discovered their shared heritage, Yolly couldn't stay away from Noemi. She hung around her, offering more juice, water, anything to keep their conversation going. After a few minutes, Bella suggested they leave Noemi to rest and find something else for Yolly to do. Yolly complied, but kept glancing over at the pregnant woman who had closed her eyes and was dozing in the chair. When she stood up a half hour later, a solicitous Yolly was at her side, helping her up, opening the door.

"Thank you," Noemi said sincerely, "it was very nice to meet you."

"Me too!" burst out the impulsive 11-year-old, who stood at the door waving good-bye until Noemi had passed the corner.

"I've never met anyone from Morocco," she said, turning to Bella, "just Daddy and his parents and they're so boring. She seems really cool!"

Much to Bella's surprise, Yolly was actually helpful. At the end of the day, she looked around the store, pleased at how much space had now been liberated from stuff she'd left lying around for too long. The cabinets had been wiped, the floor had been swept. The store looked cleaner than it had in a while. Really, that girl was amazing. When she applied her single-mindedness to a task, she could work wonders. Bella paid her what she considered a reasonable amount of money for a job well done, which, judging by Yolly's reaction, was more than adequate. She also thanked her profusely, which got almost as big a reaction as the money. Yolly gave her a huge hug before placing a licorice pipe in her mouth and descending into the metro station for the return journey.

∞

BELLA HAD A PLEASANT JOLT the next morning when she saw the new yarmulka in *objets'* window. "How lovely," she enthused. "Maybe not quite as beautiful as the other one, but pretty gorgeous!"

She admired it for a while as the voices in her head held a lively debate: *Get it, get it, you deserve it,* said the one, refuted immediately by *Whatever for? It would be senseless, what do you need that for? Buy yourself something useful if you want a present.* She listened to the two sides a little longer, thinking and maybe even hoping that the first voice would win the argument. *Yes,* whispered a third, previously silent voice, *and it would be such a neighbourly thing to do — remember she just had a break-in and robbery, you would really be helping. So buying it would even be charitable. Ha!* broke in the second voice, *How self-serving and hypocritical can you get?* At which point Bella decided it was time to go to work.

She had just begun her morning greetings when she heard the door open. She turned quickly with a smile, but found Avi rather than Daniel at the door. Luckily, he was too self-engrossed to notice how the smile faded when she saw who it was.

"Did you talk to her?"

With a little effort, Bella remembered their conversation, or rather his rant, of the week before. "No Avi, I told you I'd think about it. And I'm really not comfortable doing this. You guys need to talk to each other, not to me!"

"We've tried that. We've been doing that for a month now and we're not getting anywhere. She won't even listen to me anymore, she covers her ears and leaves the room! And she won't listen to my sister either. There's no one else I can ask, please, please," this last was said in such a plaintive manner that Bella didn't know how to refuse and found herself, once again, promising to think about it. When Noemi came in a few hours later, she thought about it for a brief moment before deciding not to mention Avi's visit. She really didn't want to get stuck between them.

Noemi looked around the store. "No cousin today?"

"No," Bella said. "I hope you didn't mind her questions. She's not exactly shy or inhibited."

"No, it was fine. It was nice to meet her, she's sweet."

"Sweet?" Not a word Bella would ever have used to describe Yolly. Although, it was true, she'd been on her best behaviour when Noemi met her.

"How are you feeling?" Bella asked.

"More pains this morning," Noemi moaned.

"Sit!" she pointed to the chair. "I'll get you something to drink."

They were sitting in companionable silence, Bella reading flower catalogues and Noemi resting with her eyes closed, when Zelda came in. Bella jumped up to greet her.

"I saw the new yarmulka in the window this morning. It's lovely."

"I'm so glad you think so. I came to see if you still want me to make you one?"

"Oh, yes, yes! At least, I think so. Maybe." Bella hesitated. She hated to bring up the subject of money when Zelda'd had so much bad luck recently, but she really didn't have much disposable income these days. Zelda didn't seem to have noticed her dithering; she was rummaging in her bag, bringing out pieces of different yarns. Bella was immediately bowled over by the magnificent colours, each one more glorious than the one before.

"Yes," she said as the first one was displayed. "Yes," to the second, and then to the third. When Zelda showed her the fourth one, she looked up pleadingly. "Please, no more, I can't take this! I can't possibly choose between them."

"I guess I'll choose for you." The crocheter laughed as she gathered up her samples. "By the way," she added, stuffing her wares into her bag, "have you seen Pedro around?"

Bella realized that she hadn't. Even though she'd found him a nuisance, she was a little miffed that he'd tired of her so quickly.

"The police were asking about him."

"Police?"

"Yes, about his figurine. They thought maybe he'd seen that dead guy before. They wanted to show him the picture, but he didn't answer their phone calls even after I told him they wanted to speak to him."

"Oh, maybe he's away then."

"Seems strange that he wouldn't take his phone though."

"Unless he's out of the country. Isn't he from South America?"

"Central, I think, El Salvador. That must be it then. Although I saw him the other day."

They were distracted by a sudden loud groan of pain from Noemi.

"What's wrong?" Alarmed, Zelda went running to the pregnant woman.

Noemi grimaced: "Apparently these are false labour pains, I've been having them for a few days and my doctor says it's nothing to worry about."

"What bullshit! These doctors know nothing. I can help you."

"And you are?" Noemi squinted at her suspiciously.

"I'm sorry, I didn't realize you hadn't met," Bella interrupted. "Noemi, this is Zelda, the owner of that store *objets*. Zelda, this is my friend Noemi who, as you can see, is very pregnant."

"I can help with your pain," Zelda repeated. "I have herbs and crystals."

"Crystals? Herbs?" asked a skeptical Noemi.

"Yes," Zelda said firmly. "Come see. You don't have to believe. It will work anyway."

Noemi looked at Bella, who nodded encouragingly. "What can it hurt?"

"Okay. I guess."

Zelda helped the pregnant woman up from her seat and they went off together. Bella watched them a little apprehensively, hoping that if Zelda really could do magic, it was only the good kind. Then she gave herself a mental shake, she didn't believe in magic! The memory of her strange attraction to the yarmulka snaked its way past her rational mind, though, and left a tiny doubt which she tried to ignore.

It was in this bemused/amused state of mind that she stopped and took a long look at the yarmulka in the window after work. The store was closed, no sign of either Zelda or Noemi. It would definitely be an extravagance, but she indulged herself so seldom. And they really were so beautiful, even if this one was not quite as exquisite as the other. And it was certainly unique. And it would doubtlessly help Zelda, who had just lost her yarmulka and, apparently, her partner. She would have to find out the price first but, if it wasn't too high, she was leaning towards yes. Even if she didn't wear it, she could hang it up and admire it on her wall.

∞

THE DEAD MAN had been identified. When they'd widened the search, Interpol had matched his fingerprints with a small time criminal in Nigeria who had been in prison until a few months ago and then dropped out of sight. The information was sketchy. Martin talked to an Interpol agent who tried to explain the complicated situation in Nigeria.

"It's volatile, a constantly shifting terrain. Who's in charge, who's out of favour, who's aligned with who, who's dead … we can't keep up with it, so I can't guarantee this information is still current. But as far as we know, the group with the most power these days is called the New Nigerian Movement, the NNM. They are partly in the open, partly hidden. They have people in the government, in the police, in the army, but they're not in control of any of those. There appear to be power struggles going on at all levels just about all the time. But the NNM has a lot of popular support because they are nationalists as well as criminals. They advocate Nigeria for Nigerians, Africa for Africans, by which they mean native Nigerians, before the colonialists came. So a lot of the tribes like them, and a lot of the anti-colonialists and anti-westerners like them."

"I've never heard of them," Martin confessed.

"That's because you're all the way over there in America. They're very powerful in Nigeria itself, and have spread throughout Africa, and they've also been making inroads into Europe, a little in Asia and a very little in South America: Brazil and Argentina. But until now, nothing in North America, at least nothing we know about."

"Just our luck!"

"Ha, ha, yes, I guess. Anyway, your dead guy's finger-prints match Toben Okonkwo, not a known member of the NNM. And not a leader type, or the brightest guy, from the court case against him, which I have in front of me and which I can send you. Until a few months ago, he was in prison with a bunch of NNMers and that's probably who he's aligned with now. I can give you his mother's contact info, but it's unlikely she's seen him, she's the one who turned him in in the first place. What do you want him for?"

"Something to do with old statues, Mayan figures ... anything like that in their portfolio?"

"Not that I know of, but they're into pretty well any-thing that makes money. In Nigeria itself, it's mostly drugs and fraud, the government even put through a special 419 law trying to put an end to their world-wide phone scams, which is very big business there. But outside of Nigeria, they do whatever works: drugs, prostitution, white slaves, smuggling, you name it. And they're not shy with their methods either, they're about as dirty and violent as they come."

"Great," was Martin's dejected response. "And now we can look forward to them here."

"So what about Okonkwo? Do you have him in jail?"

"Oh, no, sorry, I guess I didn't tell you. He's dead, un-der suspicious circumstances relating to a robbery of an antique statue."

"Oh well, no great loss. I'll move him into our inactive file."

∞

INSPECTOR MARTIN'S next stop was the hospital. He sat down in the chair next to the 15-year-old knifing victim's bed. The boy, alone in the room, was plugged into his

IPOD and didn't see him until it was too late to feign sleep. Martin motioned for him to remove the ear pods.

"Do you want to tell me what happened?" he asked.

"I don't have to tell you anything!"

"Don't you want us to find who did this to you?"

"No! It's done, it's finished, I don't care about catching them."

"Is that what your parents want too?"

The boy looked alarmed. "Yes! that's what they want. What we all want. For you to just leave us alone and forget about it."

Martin looked at him curiously. "I can't do that, it was a violent crime, you were seriously hurt."

"Well I'm okay now so just forget about it!"

"You know I'll have to talk to your parents, right?"

The boy's voice squeaked into the upper register as he struggled to maintain his belligerent tone. "Why would you do that! I'm telling you, we don't want you to investigate this!"

"Are you saying you don't want your parents present when I speak with you? You waive your right to have them here?"

"Yes! that's exactly what I'm saying!"

The inspector took out his notebook. "I'll need you to put that in writing."

"No!"

"You don't want to write it down? Would you prefer to record it?" He took out his phone.

"No! No, neither!"

"Do you want to waive your right to have your parents present or not?"

"Yes, but I don't want a record of it."

Martin shook his head. "There has to be a record. That's the way the law works."

"Then I don't waive it."

His voice had risen in pitch and volume again. A nurse poked her head in the door. "Is everything okay here?"

Martin showed his badge. "We're just having a conversation."

"Isn't he too young? Don't you need to have his parents present?"

"That's exactly what we were discussing." The detective got to his feet and nodded to the boy. "I'll be back with your parents. Don't go anywhere."

"Okay, okay, I'll sign it."

Martin, who had reached the door by this point, returned to the bed. "Are you sure? I don't want you to feel pressured."

The boy sighed. "No, it's okay. They'll find out anyways, there's no way to keep it from them."

"You mean your parents?"

He nodded dejectedly and reached for the notebook. He wrote and signed a waiver, then faced the detective as if bracing himself before a firing squad.

"So, Sébastien," Martin took the notebook back and kept it open for the questioning, "what happened to you?"

"The guy came out of nowhere. I have no idea who he was or why he attacked me. That's the truth!"

"Okay. Where were you when this happened?"

"On Park. That block with the deserted buildings."

"And ...?"

"I was just leaving."

Martin interrupted, "Leaving? Was someone else there with you?"

"Can we keep this just between the two of us? Now that I've signed your waiver, there's no need to tell my parents, right?"

He looked at him steadily. "Sébastien, what were you doing there?"

"The thing is, I don't want my parents to know...."

Martin figured a little prodding might help them move on. "Was it drugs?"

"Well, yes…. But you won't tell my parents, will you? Now that I've signed your waiver…?"

"Just tell me what happened and we'll see."

"So, I had just bought some weed … oh my god, my bag of weed! Where is it?"

"Was it on you when you were brought in?"

"I… I don't know… it was in my pocket when he attacked me.…"

"Did he stick around? Could he have taken it? Maybe that's why he attacked you?"

"No… no, he ran off right away. And then I heard glass breaking, lots of glass breaking, really loud. I… I sort of staggered over towards the sound and saw all this broken glass and I don't remember anything more really until I woke up in here.…"

"You were found two blocks away. Do you remember how you got there?"

The boy shook his head. "No, it's all a blur, everything after he knifed me. I think I was bleeding … I couldn't quite figure out what had happened.…"

"Were you high?"

When Sébastien didn't answer, Martin added, "I'm not interested in your drug doings. Unless we're talking about large dealing-type quantities?" When Sébastien emphatically shook his head, he continued, "Okay then, I don't care about the drugs, I want to know about the knifing."

When the boy nodded, he continued, "So you were high?" Sébastien nodded again.

"Okay. So take me through it, what you do remember."

"Okay.…"

"How did you get there? Did you go to buy drugs?"

"I was at a party. And I asked around and people told me I could buy some weed at that corner, that there was a dealer who hung out there."

"So you went there? How did you get there?"

"I got a ride but they didn't stick around, they were going to a club."

"And…?"

"And we smoked up to make sure the weed was good, and it was. Very!" He remembered who he was talking to and toned down the enthusiasm. "So I bought some weed and we'd finished, and the dealer left and I was going to the bus stop, and that's when he jumped me."

"Do you remember which store you were in front of at that point?"

Sébastien shook his head. "No, I wasn't looking at the stores."

"Did you see anything of your assailant?"

"No, I think he came from behind…. I just felt this pain in my side and felt someone pushing me down and when I crawled forward, there was glass, so I managed to stand up."

"What about the clay statue?"

"The what?"

"The clay figure that was stolen from the store."

"What are you talking about!"

"The broken glass came from a store window, a valuable clay statue was stolen."

"What does that have to do with me?"

"A fragment of the statue was in your pocket." Martin took out a picture of the shard. "The original's been sent for testing, this is what it looks like."

"I've never seen that before. Really! You have to believe me!"

Either the boy's a world-class actor, or he's telling the truth.

"Any idea how it got into your pocket?"

"I must have picked it up when I was crawling around or something. I really, really don't remember!" His voice was rising again with his panic, and the nurse was back.

"I'm sorry, but you will have to stop. You're upsetting the patient."

"Okay, I'm just finishing up here, just another minute, but I'll keep it quiet. I promise."

She gave him a disapproving glare and left with a warning that she'd be back.

As Martin stood up, Sébastien looked at him anxiously. "You won't tell my parents, will you? About the, you know…."

"I'm guessing they already know about the drugs. If you came in with a bag of marijuana along with your wounds, the hospital probably told them."

Sébastien looked stunned. "You think? They didn't say anything."

"Maybe they're waiting for you to recover."

"Oh! that's not good…."

"So if that's what you're worried about, you can probably stop worrying."

"Can you put in a good word for me?" he asked anxiously.

"If you help me, I'll try to help you."

"I am helping you! I have been helping you!"

Martin nodded his agreement. "Just a few more questions. What time was all this?"

"Must have been after midnight, maybe 2?"

"What about the dealer? Maybe he saw something. I'll need his name and number."

The boy looked worried at having to disappoint the detective and maybe ruin his chances at avoiding trouble. "I don't know it. I was just hanging around looking to buy … and my friends had told me to try that block, that there's usually someone there. Really! You have to believe me!"

Martin put away his notebook. "I'll check all this out and be in touch."

"You won't talk to my parents?" He seemed unable to decide which would be worse: the police talking to his parents or leaving him to face his parents alone.

"Not for the moment."

∞

NOEMI WAS SMILING the next day, looking much happier than she had for a while. "Just stopped by to tell you her magic worked!" she said. "I know. I was as surprised as you are. But I was desperate enough to let her do her thingie." She waved her hands in the air and over her belly. "She said some mumbo jumbo and waved a crystal around and gave me some horrible herbs to drink. And I slept better than I have for a long time and feel good this morning!"

"Poor woman," she continued, "she was crocheting a new kippah while I was resting after the crystal thing, and she started crying over it. She seems to have really loved the one that got stolen." Noemi shook her head at this strange attachment.

Bella understood: while undoubtedly less powerfully than Zelda, she'd also felt the pull of the yarmulka. She decided to go tell her she did want one, maybe that would cheer her up. There was just the usual reservation. Ever practical, Bella told herself the price would still have to be the deciding factor. She left Raoul at the store and went over to *objets*.

At the corner between their stores, she saw a familiar figure waiting to cross the street. She tapped her on the shoulder and was shocked by the ferocious scowl on the face that whirled round. "Oh, Bell! Oh, hi." Her high school friend's expression returned to normal so quickly she wasn't sure she'd really seen the other one.

"Emkay," she said a little cautiously, "how's it going?"

"Oh great, it's going great! How 'bout you?"

Bella was still wary. The face she'd glimpsed had scared her. "What are you up to these days?"

"Nothing much, just hanging round, waiting 'til I can get out of here." She seemed to be very jumpy, and as soon as the light changed, she hurried away

It's true, we don't have much to say to one another anymore, but that was pretty rude! More than a little offended, Bella continued on to *objets*. She got there just as a large man with 'cop' written all over him was leaving. She looked questioningly at Zelda, who shrugged helplessly.

"This just gets stranger and stranger. They've ID'ed the dead man. He's Nigerian, and apparently, a known gangster. Part of a gang in Nigeria, who call themselves the NNM, the New Nigerian Movement, who have never been seen in Canada before this. What on earth was he doing with my yarmulka?"

"Wow!" Bella agreed. "Nigeria!" Struck by a thought, she asked, "Is that where Daniel is from?"

"No," Zelda shook her head, "he's from South Africa, I think."

"Have you heard from him?"

"No, not a word." Zelda tried not to sound as worried as she was feeling. The detective had also asked about Daniel. She was so afraid there was some connection between her partner, the break-in, and the dead man that she didn't want to tell the police anything about him. If he was somehow involved, she didn't want to get him in trouble, or more trouble than he was maybe in already. She'd been worried about him before; an African showing up dead made the situation much, much more ominous .

When Bella told her why she'd come, Zelda suggested a price. Bella gulped, but she could see how much work was involved and how unique and beautiful the result. She did some mental calculations and concluded she could afford it and, what's more, she should. It was a long time since she'd bought herself a present. The dazzling smile with which Zelda greeted her decision made her very glad she'd said yes. She selected the basic colour (blue) and decorations (buttons and feathers, both small, but no sparklies) and went home, already impatient to see the finished product.

Still excited about her present to herself and pleased at her uncharacteristic daring, Bella was eager to see the window display yarmulka the next morning, even though she knew hers would be different. When she got to *objets*, she was disappointed to see an empty space where the yarmulka had been.

I guess she took it to the person who commissioned it. She was a little disappointed for herself, then brightened up: *Hopefully, she'll have trouble keeping them in stock. That will be very good for her business.*

∞

WHEN NOEMI NEXT showed up, she was crabbier than ever: the magic had worn off. "My back and feet are killing me," she told Bella, "I'm going to see if Zelda can do anything."

Bella told her about her decision to get a yarmulka. "See if she's working on it yet. I can wear it to your baby ceremony."

"Did you have to remind me?" Noemi grumbled as she left the store.

Bella looked after her in irritation. *I'll also be glad when this baby comes!*

Noemi trudged up the street, dragging her aching feet along with her. She leaned against the building at the corner for a moment to catch her breath, and caught a glimpse of a face, partially hidden inside a hoodie despite the heat.

"Hey, pupusa man," she called, "where are you running to?" Pedro twisted around.

"Oh, hello, you're the friend of Bellísima."

"I haven't seen you in a while."

"No, I've been busy. Why? Has my Bellísima missed me?"

"I don't think so!"

"Maybe you could put in a good word for me?"

Noemi laughed. "I could put in a good word for your mother!"

The exchange made her forget her pains for a moment, so she was feeling marginally better when she got to *objets*. Zelda immediately invited her in, cleared a space inside the store, and prepared a foot bath which smelled as foul as the tea she'd made the other day. Noemi didn't hesitate before gratefully sinking into the soft chair and placing her swollen feet into the basin. Zelda sat down next to her and sang softly and soothingly as she picked up her crocheting.

"Is that for Bella?" Noemi asked drowsily. Zelda doubted she was awake enough to see the answering nod. She continued crocheting. It helped soothe the worry in her heart and the pieces she made would help develop her business.

When Nurit showed up looking for her sister-in-law, Bella directed her to the narrow store down the street. She almost suggested that Nurit stop pestering Noemi, but opted against interfering. True, Noemi had been venting to her, but she wasn't part of their family, she didn't know Nurit, and it really was none of her business. In her experience, people didn't often appreciate unsolicited advice.

In fact, though, Nurit might have appreciated it this time. She walked down the block slowly, thinking she should turn around and go home. She could tell Avi she hadn't found Noemi, which was still technically true. But Noemi talked to Bella a lot and Bella might mention that she'd sent her, Nurit, to *objets*, and it would seem suspicious. She was trying very hard to stay under everyone's radar and deflect suspicion of any kind. So she urged herself on and arrived at her destination long before she was ready.

She made herself enter the store right away. As soon as her eyes adjusted to the softly-lit interior, she saw her sister-in-law reclining with eyes closed. Next to her, a grey-haired woman sat crocheting what looked like a kippah. She let out a startled gasp, which she managed to transform into a cough. She retrieved her much-improved and gratefully-pain-free sister-in-law and escorted her home. She wished she could go home herself, to England, but her parents were just about to arrive and it would look very suspicious. At this point, she just had to stay put and hope for the best. She wished the baby would get itself born already so it could all be over.

In the meantime, they had the issue of the circumcision to settle. *Why is Noemi being so difficult about this? It is so unimportant, after all, just a little snip and it's over. Why cause so much trouble?* This was not something her parents could ever go along with and it would cause endless conflict. They would never forget or forgive. *Why can't Noemi just leave it alone!*

∞

MATHIEU DIDN'T GET what the fuss was about either. Just a little cut, who cared? Ever since Nurit had shown up this evening, she'd been going on and on about it, and he was bored. Anyway, he agreed with her. He'd been circumcised, just about every man he knew had been circumcised, it's what they automatically did back then. He'd been young enough that he didn't remember it. He didn't feel like his human rights had been violated or that he'd been scarred for life by the trauma.

Finally, she seemed to have talked it out of her system. He was able to change the subject and they snuggled up together on the couch to watch the comedy show being broadcast live from the festival downtown. Usually one of Fritz's favourite shows, tonight the cat was nowhere in sight.

Week 6

From time to time, the neighbour's uncle dropped by. Still part of the rebel forces fighting in the south, he would slip in and out at night. His nieces and nephews adored him and would hardly leave him alone. While he soaked his filth-encrusted body in the bath, they would stand outside the bathroom door, playing with his gun and machete, taking great pleasure in frightening their unwanted guests, despite their mother's weak protests. Even Nando, who got along with everyone, would try and melt into the background during these episodes.

He, himself, still bore the scar from the slash he'd received the time the older daughter had been demonstrating to her siblings how to wield the machete when her hand slipped. The subsequent cut on his arm was, luckily, only superficial and the girl shamefacedly gave the weapon back to her uncle. But the reprieve was temporary. The next time her uncle appeared, she and her siblings joyfully pounced on the machete again.

The rest of their lives passed peacefully. He wanted, above all, to create a life for his little family that would have made his parents proud. The economy was booming with the influx of oil money and he was determined to make the most of the new possibilities. He worked so hard at his studies that university became a real possibility. Because the local universities had not yet recovered sufficiently from the war years, he knew he would have to study abroad. Setting his sights on England, he made sure to study English in high school. If England did not work out, the rest of the English-speaking world would still be possible.

The government also judged the local universities to be inadequate and was offering scholarships to students on condition that they return afterwards to work for the country's benefit. As a result of his persistence, and perhaps, also because of the lucky charm his mother had given him which never left his person, he was accepted to the London School of Economics to study Management. The government was impressed enough to give him a full scholarship, enough to study and to live and even a 'compassionate stipend' to come home every four months to visit his orphan brother.

∞

INSPECTOR MARTIN WAS BACK wearing a severe expression.

"What's the matter?" Zelda asked, apprehensive. "You look like it's bad news."

"Have you heard from your partner?"

"Not a word." Her breath caught and she asked, "You haven't found another body, have you?"

"No, but we have been making inquiries."

"You've found out more about the Nigerians?"

"Not much. But we haven't been able to find any record at all, anywhere, of Daniel Monroe. Not here or through Interpol."

"Why are you looking for Daniel?"

"He went missing at the same time. We would like to talk to him, to see if he saw or heard anything suspicious."

He didn't add, but Zelda heard it clearly: *or if he is involved in this.*

"I'm sorry," she said, "I really don't know much about him."

"He was your partner?"

"Well, yes, but not legally. The store's all mine. But he helped with all the work."

"How long have you known him?"

"A little over a year, I guess."

"Where did you meet him?"

"Well, he just showed up. It was at the occult fair." At the questioning look, she explained: "Every year, at the exhibition centre…. We have a booth there, my coven."

"Your what?"

Zelda decided to forego the details about her Wiccan practice: "My friends and I. A booth, where we sell things."

"And you met Daniel there?"

"Yes, he came by and we started talking. He was very interested in what we do so I invited him to come to our next meeting. He joined our coven, our group, and we became friends."

"And he told you his name was Daniel Monroe?" At her nod, he continued, "Did you ever see any kind of identification?"

"No. Who asks for ID? A person says their name is Daniel and of course you believe them. Why would someone lie about that?"

"That's a very good question," said the detective. "Why would he? Do you know where he's from?"

"No," she shook her head, "he never said. Although I had the impression it was South Africa."

"But you never asked?"

She shook her head.

"So it could be Nigeria?"

"I guess ...."

"The address you gave me for him is the only you have?" When she nodded, he said, "It appears to have been cleared out." At her slight gasp, he nodded, "Yes. It looks like he's not coming back."

He had no more questions. As he stood to go, he said, "You have my card. You will let me know if you hear from him or about him?"

"Yes," she replied, still reeling from the revelations.

"And this other guy, the owner of the statue? I haven't been able to get hold of him either, he hasn't returned my calls. Do you know where he is?"

"No, I haven't seen him lately either. I told him you wanted to see him, maybe he's away."

∞

CARL WAS SITTING at a desk trying to finish the day's paper-work when Stéphane Martin approached. "Sorry to inter-rupt," the inspector began.

"Not a problem." Carl pushed the pile away.

Martin smiled, acknowledging a shared dislike of that aspect of their jobs, and continued: "About your break-in? The one with the knitted hat? Looks like it's tied to Nige-rian gangsters."

At Carl's obvious interest, the Inspector filled him in on the little they knew. "Ever think about becoming an in-spector?" he asked before returning to his own pile of pa-pers. "That was a good reading on the piece of statue – we could use smart people like you."

Carl sat there for a moment, savouring the compliment, pondering the question. Maybe he should think about it. At this point, anything to occupy his thoughts would be welcome. Over a week had passed since he'd received Jake's letter, over a week in which he'd successfully avoided thinking about it. He'd had years of practice in not thinking about things, but banishing Jake from his thoughts hadn't worked out all that well: his dreams had begun to deal with the issue his waking mind refused to face – whether or not to respond. He'd had dreams in which he did respond and dreams in which he didn't, both had turned into night-mares. He'd begun to dread sleeping and was staying up too late and drinking too much. Inspector-training would be a good career move and, hopefully, would demand all his attention, both conscious and unconscious.

∞

YOLLY HAD TALKED her way into visiting Bella a second time. Her family was going to the country for two weeks and she didn't want to go with them. What she wanted, what she really wanted, was to continue her investigation. Or, rather, to start it, because she'd been so caught up with the excitement of being in the city that she'd forgotten about 'her case'. Sherlock Holmes would not approve.

She put on her father's winter hat – although much too big for her as well as much too warm for the summer heat, with its earflaps it was the closest thing in the house to a deerstalker. She pulled down the flaps, summoned Sherlock's spirit, and concentrated. *Aha! I'll work for Auntie Bella again! I'll make it worth it for her. And she won't even have to pay me this time. Just feed me, I guess. But that's okay, I won't eat much. Or be any trouble. So it will be SO worth her while.*

Her parents were not impressed, however, with either the hat engulfing half her head or the plan. In fact, they were so adamant in their refusal that she knew not to waste time trying to change their minds. Instead, after communing with her Sherlock spirit, she came running back with an alternative: her father had some work he couldn't put off, so he would be going up a couple of days later. Yolly could spend those two days with Bella and come up with George. While not ideal, at least it would give her two days to investigate, which might be enough if she was really diligent. To Lila's surprise, and even to Yolly's, Bella seriously considered and then granted the request. It was true, Yolly had been a real help, and Bella was still enjoying the tidier store.

Bella picked up her cousin (who for some unfathomable reason was wearing a winter hat much too big for her) at the same rendezvous point on the Monday and brought her to Belles Fleurs. Although it was still more orderly than it had been before her first visit, Yolly took one look around, then set about cleaning while Bella did the books. When they were both finished, the store was spotless and they both admired the sparkling effect.

The workday done, Bella was at a loss. She didn't have any experience entertaining pre-teens and was pretty sure several hours spent in her apartment would lead to extreme boredom. So, after they'd deposited Yolly's backpack on the couch which would be her bed, she took her downstairs to meet Mathieu and Fritz. Mathieu took so long answering the bell that they were just about to give up on him.

"Oh sorry, I didn't know you had company!" Bella caught a glimpse of Nurit behind her neighbour and began to draw back. But Yolly was distracted by Fritz, who had also come to the door. When she saw him, she squealed in delight and immediately flopped to the ground, made eye contact, and reached out to scratch him behind the ears. The answering purr left no doubt about the cat's feelings on the matter.

"My cousin Yolly," Bella said to Mathieu. "I'm so sorry we disturbed you. I just wanted to introduce you and Fritz."

"Looks like they've introduced themselves," he gazed at the happy couple on the ground.

While they stood on the doorstep, their neighbours Sophie and Michael appeared on the landing next door. When Michael spotted Mathieu, his face lit up and he ran down the stairs, stopping short when he saw Yolly welcoming Fritz onto her lap. He hesitated, his face reflecting his uncertainty. His shyness, which had greatly diminished this past year but could still ambush him, flooded back.

Mathieu beckoned the boy over and gathered him into a big bear hug. "When did you get back? Fritz and I have missed you!"

Bella was hit by a wave of guilt. She'd meant to stay in closer contact with Michael and his mother, but somehow a year had passed since his father'd died. The death had occurred around the same time she'd bought into Belles Fleurs, and that had occupied almost all her thoughts ever since. She hadn't even known they were away.

Michael's pleasure at Mathieu's welcome shone from his face as he returned the hug. "Just today," he replied as his mother joined them.

"Welcome back," Mathieu greeted Sophie with a two cheek kiss.

"Thank you," she smiled, "it was nice to be on vacation, but it's good to be home."

By this time, Nurit had come to the doorway which Mathieu had vacated. Bella noticed her and nudged Mathieu, motioning towards the door with her head: "Did you forget something?"

He looked where she was pointing. "Oh my god! Nurit, I'm so sorry, I got caught up in all this .... Come, come meet my neighbours." With a sweep of his arm, he named them: "Bella you know. This is Sophie," Sophie nodded hello; "Michael," Michael turned red but managed to give a small nod; "and Yolly." Yolly looked up when she heard her name. "Huh?" When she saw they were all looking at her, she remembered to be on her best behaviour and hurriedly got to her feet, transferring the cat from lap to arms.

"Huh?" she repeated, and instantly amended this to: "Excuse me? I missed that." Bella laughed to herself at Yolly's ongoing transformation from brat to polite young woman, but kept silent as Mathieu resumed the introductions. "And this is Nurit," he finished, putting an arm around the woman who looked uncomfortable with this public display of intimacy.

Mathieu didn't seem to notice her discomposure, his attention was on Michael and making sure the 12-year-old was at ease. He looked at Fritz, purring away in Yolly's arms with eyes closed. Removing his arm from Nurit, he sat down on the step and motioned to both children to join him.

"Fritz likes both of you, so you will like each other," he said firmly. "Sit down and get acquainted." He got up to make room for them. They followed his orders and, with the cat happily ensconced between them, began a halting conversation.

Mathieu rejoined the adults. Sophie said admiringly, "I don't know how you manage it, Mathieu, you're so good with him." And Bella added a heartfelt "Thank you. I didn't know what to do with her! I don't have anything for kids."

"Do you want to have dinner together?" Sophie asked "Looks like it would be good for all of us. I just went shopping, come eat with us." Bella and Sophie started to work out plans for supper and looked at Mathieu to check if he wanted to be included. He shook his head, having seen from a glance at Nurit that the idea didn't appeal to her.

"No thanks, I think we'll just return to ...," he realized he didn't want to finish the sentence, especially not with kids nearby, so he just left it at that and tried not to notice their smirks as he and Nurit went back inside.

"Is it okay if Fritz comes with us?" Bella called out, but Mathieu's door had already closed behind them.

Surprisingly, the two children, so different in temperament, hit it off. As the adults lingered at the table after supper, they retreated to Michael's room when he tentatively offered to show Yolly his first graphic novel attempts and she enthusiastically accepted. Fritz, realizing his fans had abandoned him, opened his eyes, stood, stretched, and went running to find them.

"How long is she staying with you?"

"Just until tomorrow. Her father's coming to take her up to the country to join the rest of her family. She wanted to come here instead of going with them."

"Another city girl!"

"I think so – she likes excitement. Wants to be a detective, investigate our local break-in."

At Sophie's questioning look, Bella realized she knew nothing about the new store and recent neighbourhood events, so she brought her up to date.

"Sounds like an interesting store," was Sophie's comment.

"You should see the things they have, even yarmulkas! She's making one for me."

"For you? A yarmulka?" The two years she'd known her were enough for Sophie to have noticed Bella's lacklustre interest in anything remotely Jewish.

"Yes, believe it or not! These are like nothing I've seen before, they don't look like yarmulkas at all!"

Bella interrupted the children when it was time to leave. Their disappointed faces showed the extent to which they'd bonded. Fritz followed them out and down the stairs, then scratched at the door to his own abode as Bella and Yolly climbed the stairs to theirs.

∞

YOLLY WOKE UP with a start the next morning. She'd been so occupied the day before, what with one thing and another, that she'd forgotten her investigation. She didn't have much time – her father would be coming in the afternoon – and she determined to make the most of what she had left.

She had Bella show her the site of the break-in on their walk to work. Later, when she was sure Bella was busy in the back, she pulled the hat down over her eyes, stuck the somewhat-chewed licorice pipe in her mouth, and snuck out of the flower store. She was careful to look both ways before crossing the quiet street between the blocks, then hesitated when she saw there was someone at her destination. She hung back. When the interloper didn't move on right away, she took cover around the corner.

Yuck! She'd stepped into a pile of ashes and butts. *People are such pigs!*

She lifted her foot to shake off the rubbish and realized it was pot, leftover roaches, not just tobacco butts. Even in her suburban elementary school, she'd been exposed to enough of both to know the difference. She stared down, wondering if this could be related to her case at all.... Determined to leave no possible clue unexplored, she picked up one of the roaches, using a corner of her shirt to make sure she didn't contaminate the evidence, and placed it carefully in her pocket. She heard a car and remembered her mission.

Oh my god! I forgot! Sorry, Sherlock, I know I have to do better. Keep my eyes on the target!

She ran back towards the corner, slamming on the brakes when she realized that the person outside *objets* was still there. The situation required careful reconnaissance and analysis. She considered the possibility that this was a homeless person. She'd never actually seen one, but this woman was just hanging around on the street, not going anywhere. However, she didn't resemble what Yolly'd seen on TV: she was dressed okay and lacked accompanying shopping cart or bags. Furthermore, she seemed to be engaged in the same kind of snooping that Yolly had intended to do herself. So, not a homeless person. But who was she? And why was she there?

As she watched, the woman finished searching the sidewalk around the store and crossed the street. Yolly got ready to take her place, but the woman took up her scrutiny on the other side. Yolly shrank back, just in time, as the woman looked around and, satisfied that she was not being observed, picked up something from the seam between the sidewalk and vacant building. After checking again to make sure she was alone, she quickly put the hand containing the something into her pocket. When she removed it, Yolly could see that it was empty. And, now that she could see the woman's face clearly, she recognized the woman who'd been with Bella's downstairs neighbour the night before.

Realizing that she'd been gone longer than she'd intended and that she'd better get back before Bella had a fit, she crossed the still unbusy street, after carefully checking for cars, and ran back to the flower store. Bella had, in fact, just realized she wasn't there and started yelling at her right away. All ideas of 'best behaviour' forgotten, Yolly yelled over her. Her news was too important to wait.

"Auntie Bella, Auntie Bella, I saw her. I saw that woman from yesterday. At the break-in store. She found something on the sidewalk. And put it in her pocket. She looked really guilty, she even checked to see if anyone was watching before she picked it up. And again before she put it in her pocket. You know, the woman from yesterday. With your neighbour, the one with the cat."

She succeeded in getting through to Bella, who cut short her diatribe to listen to the words pouring out of her cousin.

"Do you mean Nurit?" she asked, incredulous. "She was with Mathieu."

"Yes! That's the one! She was there just now and she found something. At the break-in store. No, not at the store. Across the street. But first she checked out the whole space around the store. Then she crossed the street and kept searching. I saw her!"

"What did she find?" Bella resorted to the same technique she'd perfected to interrupt her mother's non-stop monologues – she just started speaking over the endless word stream.

"I don't know, I couldn't see, but it fit in her pocket. She checked that no one was looking, I was hiding around the corner, and then she put it in her pocket."

"And before that she was looking at *objets*? The store that was broken into?"

"Yes! That's what I'm trying to tell you!"

"I'm sure she was just looking for something she lost. Maybe an earring or a button."

"Maybe...." Doubt crept into Yolly's voice. She paused, stooped to pick up the licorice pipe that had fallen to the ground in her excitement, wiped it on her clothes, and stuck it back in her mouth. Bella tried not to shudder. "Don't you think it's suspicious? Like she was the perp and returned to the scene of the crime to make sure she'd covered her trail?"

At that, Bella laughed, "Or maybe you've watched too many detective shows?"

When Yolly's face crumpled at the belittling of her detectiving abilities, Bella felt bad and tried to reverse the effect: "But I'll make sure to ask her next time I see her."

"I guess," said Yolly grudgingly, hardly mollified.

Bella's conscience pushed her to compensate: "And I'll let you know. Okay?"

At that, Yolly's face lit up, returning to its former intensity. "As soon as you find out!" she demanded. "You'll call me, even if I'm in the country?"

"Okay," Bella promised, not wanting to trigger a new round of misery.

"Oh, I almost forgot. I also found drugs." This finally earned her Bella's complete, concentrated, attention. "Marijuana butts, roaches. Around the corner. A pile of them."

"Are you sure it wasn't tobacco?" At Yolly's contemptuous roll of the eyes, Bella began to worry. If her cousin was into drugs already, she had to tell her parents. "How do you know what marijuana looks like?"

"From school. People smoke."

"11-year-olds?"

"Yah. Not me, though, I'm not that stupid! Here, I brought one back."

Again being careful not to get her fingerprints on the evidence, she pulled the butt out with a corner of her shirt. "Do you have an evidence bag?" she asked importantly.

"I'm sorry, I'm all out of those. But I do have a baggie, will that do?" Yolly ignored the sarcasm and reached for the baggie, into which she carefully inserted what she referred to as 'the evidence.' Bella, confused, asked, "What do you think this is evidence of?"

"It might have the perp's fingerprints or DNA on it! Maybe he smoked it while he was waiting for the coast to be clear."

"I suppose it's possible...."

"We need to get it analyzed!" Bella was still thinking about the 'we' of the plan when Yolly, inspired, declared, "We need to give it to Uncle Carl!"

Uh oh, that 'we' has just expanded to include Carl as well.

"Oh no!" Yolly's wail quickly refocused Bella's attention. "What's the matter? What is it?"

"I won't be here – I have to go to the country!" The wail threatened to become a full-blown tantrum. "I can't go, I can't! This is too important, this is two clues that need following up! I can't leave now!"

Knowing that Lila and George wouldn't thank her if she returned their daughter in this condition, but also sure she would regret it, she heard herself promising to follow up for her.

The tears were immediately replaced by a smile. "You promise? You'll call Carl? About that woman and about the pot? You'll give him the evidence?"

At this point, Bella could only nod her head, confirming that she would do all that.

"And you'll report back to me?"

"Yolly!" she tried to remonstrate at this exigency, but Yolly repeated, "You'll report back? I need to know I can trust you with this!"

Unwilling to engage in a power struggle with the determined 'detective', Bella thought it simpler to just agree. "Yes," she sighed, "I'll let you know."

The "Thank you, Auntie Bella! You're the best!" was accompanied by a bear hug and a huge smile. Bella knew she'd been skillfully manipulated, but smiled back anyway, shaking her head gently. "It's a good thing I love you!"

When George came to pick up his daughter, Yolly launched into her story immediately, giving him a somewhat expanded version and going into great detail. She broke this off to remind Bella of her promise to phone "AS SOON" as she had any news, then went back to telling her father all about her case. She had to run back in for her deerstalker hat, then again to hug Bella goodbye. Finally, they drove away.

Bella didn't see Nurit that day, but Mathieu dropped by in the late afternoon on his way home from work.

"Just wanted to explain about yesterday."

"No explanation necessary," Bella assured him.

"I don't want you to get the wrong idea, or think I'm getting unfriendly or anything!"

"I think we got the right idea, that what you were getting was lucky!" she smirked.

He squirmed slightly, just enough to confirm her supposition. "She's amazing," he started to say, "I've never met anyone like her…"

"…Speaking of Nurit," Bella remembered her promise and interrupted him, "Yolly, my little cousin, you remember meeting her last night? or did you have eyes only for Nurit…?"

"Ha, ha, very funny! Yes, I remember, Fritz liked her."

"Well, Yolly saw Nurit find something on the sidewalk around *objets* and put it in her pocket. This morning. Sort of secretively."

Mathieu looked skeptical. "I can't imagine what that's about. Is she sure it was Nurit?"

"She was sure. And she's very observant – she's training herself to be a detective and she prides herself on what she calls her 'detectiving' skills. There's a chance she was mistaken, but she's usually right. If she says she saw Nurit pick something up, she probably did."

"I'll ask Nurit."

"Let me know, I promised to keep her posted. Oh! and she also found some marijuana butts around the corner. She brought me one to have analyzed in case it has the 'perp's' DNA on it!" Bella held up the makeshift evidence bag. "I promised to pass it on to my brother. But isn't that where you thought you saw the drug dealing the other day?"

"Just about…. Looks like we'll have to start the patrols again."

"I guess it was too good to last. It's been a while since our last cleanup."

They both sighed gloomily at the thought of restarting the drug patrols.

"Are you leaving now? We could walk home together."

"Sorry, I still have a couple of things to do. Maybe I'll see you later?"

"Maybe, but I'm supposed to see Nurit…."

"Oh well, in that case," she smirked again. Mathieu smiled uncomfortably, happy to have found Nurit but not wanting it to interfere with his friendships. He started to explain all this to Bella as she laughed at him.

"Go! Enjoy! I'll still be here when you come up for air."

∞

WHEN BELLA GOT HOME the next evening, there was already a message on her voicemail: "Well? What'd Uncle Carl say? You forgot to call me! What'd that woman say? What was it she found?" and, after a moment's silence, "This is Yolly," then click.

Good god, it had only been one day! She could imagine the torrent of phone calls that would come her way if she didn't act quickly. So she punched in Mathieu's number.

"Sorry to bug you but Yolly is already bugging me," she said to his voicemail – this was a slight exaggeration, true, but it didn't take Zelda's magic to foretell her future – "about her detectiving. Did you ask Nurit about it? Let me know if you did, what she said. Thanks. If it's not too much trouble, in between your other activities!" she added before hanging up. *Really! The things that girl is pushing me into. I'll soon become the neighbourhood gossip if this keeps up.*

∞

"SHE'S WRONG! Stupid little nosy snoop!" Mathieu stared at Nurit, dumbfounded by the vehemence of her response. He'd forgotten all about Yolly's supposed observation until he listened to Bella's message. Relaxing on the couch after the excellent supper the local diner had cooked, he'd mentioned it as a joke, expecting Nurit to laugh with him at the young detective; instead she'd erupted.

He tried to soothe her: "Well of course she got it wrong! Why ever would you be searching the sidewalk? She obviously has a very active imagination. We should get her to write novels."

His attempt to distract Nurit failed, she remained agitated all evening. She brushed off his concerned queries with a brusque "Nothing's wrong!" and when he touched her shoulder from behind, jumped in alarm. He woke a few hours later to an empty bed and creaking sounds from the kitchen. Concerned about Nurit and wanting to make sure a midnight contretemps with Fritz didn't exacerbate her aggravation, he got up to check on things.

Fritz was nowhere in sight, his (fortunate or unfortunate, depending on your point of view) usual state when Nurit was around. Mathieu reached the kitchen just in time to see her stuff a piece of paper into the garbage can in what he could only describe as a stealthy manner. He waited until she stood up, then entered the room.

"Oh hi, Mathieu. I just came for a glass of water," she said, a little too quickly.

"Good idea after all the that wine and food," he agreed and joined her at the sink.

He managed to contain his curiosity until the next morning. Then, after they'd left together and reached the corner, he suddenly 'remembered' a book he needed for work and they parted, she to wander, he to return home alone.

Once there, he eyed the garbage can, unsure how to proceed. Luckily, because of recycling and composting, his actual garbage was small, although the leftovers from last night's souvlakis, combined with Fritz's waste products, were already fragrant. He found a large plastic garbage bag, spread it out on the floor and, holding his breath, upended the garbage onto it. Revolted by the thought of plunging his hands into the smelly pile, he fetched his gardening gloves and, thus protected, started sifting through it.

He had no idea what he was looking for, just anything that looked out of place. The only thing he found that could possibly qualify was a scrap of paper with *GABRIEL* written in large capital letters. It meant nothing to him – he didn't know anyone with that name, couldn't remember ever meeting anyone with that name. All he could come up with was the archangel Gabriel, whom he hadn't encountered since his childhood Sunday school.

He went through the garbage again, but there really didn't appear to be anything else. *I guess this is it, or maybe she already retrieved whatever she put there.* It was only after he'd bundled up the garbage and disposed of it in the garbage bin outside that he realized he'd forgotten about the scrap of paper, which was sitting on the counter. Caught between two plastic wrappers, it had avoided contamination from the dirty garbage in which it had been submerged, so he put it in his junk drawer and went to work.

∞

ALTHOUGH SHE'D SEARCHED pretty thoroughly, Nurit hadn't found anything other than a scrap of paper with Gabriel's name written on it. A name that would have been meaningless to anyone else. But, just to be sure, she'd taken it, just in case the scrap should fall into the hands of the police and, by some unforeseeable chain of events, become meaningful to them. This was not going well, at all! She felt like her life had taken a nosedive. She'd been making wrong decisions, one after the other. Everything was going wrong. Well, maybe not everything, there was Mathieu, but he'd been an oasis in the middle of a disaster-desert. Maybe she should have left the scrap of paper where it was; the word *Gabriel* would have been insignificant to everyone here. She wasn't thinking clearly anymore – she really needed to get away but that stupid baby hadn't arrived yet!

∞

SOPHIE POKED HER HEAD into Belles Fleurs. She'd begun to do the books for a number of smaller businesses. Most of this she did at home, which allowed her to be there when Michael came home from school. Life as a single parent was not turning out to be as difficult as she'd feared. Back from vacation, she was making the rounds of her clients to collect their recent paperwork.

When she saw the bromeliad in full bloom, she came all the way in and went over to it, stopped and closed her eyes, breathing in the fragrance of the red flower. "Wow! Is that new?" Sophie was an enthusiastic gardener, although not as knowledgeable as Mathieu, who had taken her under his gardening wing.

Bella nodded. "Yes, I just found a local supplier. It's nice, isn't it?"

"Nice doesn't even begin to describe it!" Sophie inhaled the aroma again. "Did your cousin leave?"

At Bella's nod, Sophie continued, "Too bad, I was going to invite you guys for dinner, she and Michael got along so well."

"That was actually the first time she's been to my house."

"She seemed very sweet."

"I know – I was so surprised!" At Sophie's reaction, she explained, "She's not usually quite so sweet, this is recent."

"Michael liked her and he doesn't like many people, he's still very shy."

They'd discussed this shyness before and Bella knew Sophie was encouraging him to talk to people: "Maybe I'll invite her over again. I'll let you know."

Noemi made her daily appearance at that point. Sophie, who hadn't seen her for a while, grinned at the protruding belly. "Won't be long now!"

"I hope not," moaned Noemi. "Can't come soon enough."

"Yes, I remember," sympathized Sophie. "I was also pregnant through a hot summer: Michael is a September baby. Do you know if it's a boy or a girl?"

Bella left them to chat. Gathering her trimming implements, she started making her way methodically through the store, checking each plant and pruning where necessary.

Meanwhile Noemi explained the circumcision problem to Sophie, who'd sat down in Bella's chair so the other woman didn't have to crane her neck.

"I've never heard of Jews not circumcising," she said wonderingly. "Are there many who don't?"

"Not so many, but a growing number who object to the sexism of marking the Jewish symbol on men only." She was pleased to see that Sophie knew what this meant. "Then there's also the child mutilation aspect, which lots of doctors say is not healthy, the opposite of what they used to think."

"Wow. Who knew? When Michael was born, we did it automatically, with a *mohel* and everything."

"Yes, that's what Avi wants." Her sigh shook her entire body.

Sophie stood up. "Sorry, I'd love to stay and talk but I have to get to work."

"That's okay, thanks for listening."

After she'd finished pruning, Bella sat down next to a dozing Noemi. By the time she finished opening the mail, Noemi's eyes were open.

"More pain?" Bella asked.

"Not today. Just the feet. When I can stand, maybe I'll go see if Zelda can give me some herbs for them. I'm beginning to believe that she really is a witch."

"If so, maybe her magic can help with the circumcision problem too."

"There's a thought. She is Jewish, I think."

"Do you know how that can be?" Bella remembered her initial curiosity when Daniel had told her about their being Wiccan. "How she can be Jewish and Wiccan?"

"I have no idea, you should ask her. And I think I *will* ask her about the circumcision. I have a feeling she wouldn't be in favour of cutting, maybe she can think of ways to convince Avi."

"He and Nurit haven't backed off at all?" Bella had decided to not tell Noemi that Avi'd asked her to intervene, she was afraid that confessing would land her squarely in the middle that she was trying to avoid.

"No, but it's just been him, I haven't seen much of Nurit lately."

"I think she's been at Mathieu's."

The words were out of her mouth before she could censor them. *Oh no! I'm becoming a gossip!*

Noemi was looking inquiringly at her. "Oh, yes?"

Bella couldn't not continue at this point, so she nodded reluctantly. "I saw her there a few nights ago."

"So that's where she's been!"

"Not when she went AWOL, I don't think." Again, she'd spoken without thinking and found herself having to go into more detail. "Mathieu didn't know where she was then either."

Once loosened, Bella's tongue seemed to have a life of its own, maybe enjoying the novelty after years of being so severely reined in. Before Bella realized what was happening, she was also telling Noemi about Yolly's discovery. At least she'd succeeded in distracting Noemi from her own problems.

"Wow!" was the response. "What do you think she found?"

Bella shrugged her ignorance. "I promised Yolly I'd follow up and I knew she'd nag, so I asked Mathieu." At Noemi's questioning look, she finished with "Haven't heard back from him, but Yolly's already called to remind me! That girl never forgets or lets up."

"Well, me neither. I'm going to ask Zelda about the circumcision. Maybe she can wave her magic wand over Avi," Noemi said as she went off to get more herbs for her aching feet.

∞

MATHIEU WAS TROUBLED when he came into the store as Bella was closing up. "I wanted to talk to you for a minute before going home."

Bella gestured toward her visitor's chair and, after locking the door and flipping the sign to '*closed*,' came and sat down beside him.

"What's the matter?"

"I got your message," he began hesitantly.

"Okay…"

"And I asked Nurit …"

She nodded.

"The thing is …, it's a little weird, … probably nothing …."

She nodded again.

"I don't know, but it seems a little strange …. I asked Nurit about what Yolly saw."

Again he hesitated, so Bella nodded yet again. Encouragingly. This was unlike Mathieu, who was usually more articulate. He took a deeper breath, then got to the point, although still a little hesitantly.

"I thought she'd laugh but she got mad instead and said Yolly was obviously making up stories and was totally mistaken. Okay, I thought, so for some reason it hit a sensitive spot. But then in the middle of the night, she got up and stuffed something into the garbage can sort of furtively."

"Oh!"

"Yes, oh."

"So you didn't see what it was?"

"Well, maybe." His cheeks reddened. "I looked. The next day. But all I found was a scrap of paper with the word *GABRIEL.*"

"Oh! Word or name?"

"No idea, it was in block letters."

"Do you know anyone named Gabriel?"

He shook his head. "No one."

"Well, if she found the paper around the store, maybe Zelda does. Noemi was on her way over there a while ago, maybe she knows a Gabriel that Nurit knows. If she's still there, we could ask them both." Her privacy concerns clicked back on and she added, "Without telling them why we're asking."

Mathieu nodded his agreement. "And I can finally meet her."

"You haven't met her yet?" Bella could barely remember a time when Zelda and her store hadn't been part of her life, but it really was only a few weeks. And Mathieu had been away when they'd opened. It was strange to have people around whom he didn't know – it was usually the reverse, with him introducing everyone to her.

"Speaking of which, I met an old friend of yours the other day."

Uh oh … only one old friend around that he hasn't met. And something about his voice sounds like this wasn't a good experience. "You met Emkay?"

"I did, she was in the park giving cigarettes to kids!"

"That's not good."

"No! And when I said that, she just laughed!"

Bella squirmed a little at her friend's disapproving tone. "I don't know her very well any more, it's been years since we were friends. From the little I've seen of her now, she doesn't seem to have changed much since high school. She makes me feel old and mature!"

"That's exactly how she made me feel!"

By this time, they'd arrived at their destination. Zelda welcomed them warmly; she'd been looking forward to meeting Mathieu. But he was preoccupied, so they moved quickly from pleasantries to the purpose of their visit.

Both women shook their heads when asked if they knew a Gabriel, and Noemi asked if this was related to Yolly's discovery. This reminded Bella of her former indiscretion and she had no choice now but to repeat the story to Zelda. Increasingly uncomfortable with her role as the spreader of tales, Bella swore them both to secrecy. Neither woman could think of any reason why Nurit would hide the piece of paper.

"Maybe she's just secretive in general," Bella finally suggested.

"Well, that's certainly true," Noemi concurred, "she never talks about what she does or where she goes or anything. At least, not to Avi or me."

"That must be it!" Relieved, Mathieu stood up. "Thank you all for listening."

"Wait up, I'll walk home with you," Bella said and they bid good night to the other two, who stayed to finish tending to Noemi's feet.

"Probably better not to mention this to Nurit," she continued as they made their way up the street.

Mathieu agreed. He liked Nurit a lot and had fantasies of their relationship stretching on into the future. Sure, she had some weird stuff, but who didn't! It was probably because they didn't know each other all that well yet. Maybe they should go out for a romantic candle-lit dinner....

∞

THEY SPLIT UP at the corner, Mathieu heading towards home while Bella continued on to Chang's, the local grocery store. Just as she got there, she was almost knocked over by a hoodied man coming out of the alley. "Watch where you're going!" she yelled as she swerved to avoid him.

At the sound of her voice, his head swung round. "Bellísima! My darling Bellísima!"

Oh no. Just my luck. "Oh, it's you, Pedro! How are you?"

"I've missed you! The sound of your voice, the shape of your body …. Have you come to have dinner with me?"

Anxious to distract him, Bella changed the subject. "Where've you been? Zelda was looking for you."

"She was? Does she have the insurance money?"

"I don't know, she didn't say. Just that she wondered where you'd gotten to."

"And dinner?" He looked at her hopefully.

"Sorry," she was saying as she climbed the stairs, and was through the door before he could respond.

Remembering that Mathieu had run into Emkay in the park, she took that route herself to get home. Sure enough, her old friend was ensconced on a bench, looking completely at home. *She can't be living here, can she? She did say she was staying with her parents.*

"Emkay, hi."

"Bel! How great to see you!" Emkay put her arms around her and kissed both her cheeks,

She's certainly friendlier than the other day! "You're not sleeping here, are you? You do have somewhere to stay?"

Emkay laughed and then laughed some more. "You're worried about me, that's so sweet!"

"Are you?" Bella was starting to get seriously worried.

"No, no, don't worry, I'm staying with my parents."

"Okay, because you're around here a lot.…"

"My parents' house is not that much fun … if you remember …. They haven't changed at all!"

I do remember; it's true, they were always on at her about not behaving herself. And she hasn't changed much either!

"I met your friend the other day."

"Mathieu? Yes, he told me."

"He didn't like me much."

Bella felt she had to defend him. "That's not true! He just didn't like you giving cigarettes to kids."

"What an old fart! Didn't he have any fun when he was young? You and I certainly did!"

"We didn't know then what we know now...."

"Oh my god – you've turned into an old fart too! Bel, Bel, Bel, what the hell happened to you? You need to start hanging out with me more, cut loose!"

Was I really like that when I was young? Or has Emkay actually de-matured in the meantime? She's so juvenile!

"Yah, well...." Bella gathered up her groceries and stood up.

"Okay, well, see you around." Emkay had her phone out before Bella even turned away.

∞

"ZELDA! Where are you? Zelda!"

Deja-vu. Yet again, she came running from the back room to find Pedro standing and hollering in the middle of the store.

"What is it? What's the matter? I was just closing up."

"I thought you wanted me! Bellísima said you were looking for me. Did you get the insurance money?"

"No, not yet, but I sent them your papers so, hopefully, it won't be long now. It was Inspector Martin who was looking for you. You know, the police officer doing the investigating. I think he wants to show you the picture of the dead man, to see if you've ever seen him, maybe hanging round or eyeing your figurine or something."

"Can you tell him for me that I don't know the guy?"

"How do you know? You haven't seen the picture. What's the matter with you, Pedro?" She was losing patience with him.

"Nothing, nothing."

∞

"WHO'S GABRIEL?" Noemi asked her sister-in-law that evening as they were eating dinner. Nurit was, an unusual occurrence, home for dinner. She turned bright red and choked on her food. When she'd stopped coughing, she saw Noemi still looking at her questioningly.

"Sorry, sorry, something caught in my throat. What were you saying?" she asked in her most innocent tone.

"Gabriel. Who is that?"

"I have no idea. Why do you ask?"

Avi looked up. "Wasn't that the name of the guy you were seeing in England when I came to visit that time?" At her blank look, he added, "The one from Africa."

Nurit shook her head. "No, his name was Nelson," she said quickly. She turned back to Noemi. "I don't think I know anyone called Gabriel," and repeated, "Why do you ask?"

Noemi said, "Just something I heard today, about someone named Gabriel," reluctant to admit that they'd been talking about her, especially since Mathieu had been involved. Noemi had a feeling he wouldn't want Nurit to know that.

Nurit left the table soon after and went into the baby-to-be's room, which was hers at the moment, closing the door behind her. Once she knew she was not being observed, her self-control crumbled; she broke into a sweat and sat down before her shaking legs collapsed. This was getting worse and worse, she didn't know how she was going to retrieve the situation. She had to try, before she was completely ruined.

She got out the burner phone and used it to call the number she'd originally been given. She didn't know if the number was still active, but it was the only one she had; she'd been told not to use it again, but she was desperate. When it had rung five times without being answered, she disconnected quickly.

Trying to figure out a plan, she began to pace.

∞

INSPECTOR MARTIN LOOKED UP from his report when he heard the phone ring. He'd forgotten about it and had to search under the stacks of accumulated papers before he located it, by which time it had long stopped ringing. He checked the call history. The calling number hadn't been blocked, so he pressed the dial key.

"Hello!" hollered a woman's voice. "Where are you?"

He wasn't sure how to best answer. If this was an innocent caller, it didn't matter much what he said, but if it was someone involved with the man's death, this was his chance to make some progress on this case. So he muttered "Hi" in a low indistinct voice and waited, hoping she'd say something else. After about 10 seconds, she said, "Who is this?" He answered, "It's me," in the same low voice. She hung up immediately, without saying another word. He pressed redial, the line rang and rang, then was abruptly disconnected. He hurried over to their tech wiz.

"This phone just rang, the one from the dead Nigerian. Any way you can trace that call?"

"Not specifically, but I'll try to pinpoint the area it came from."

He came back to the inspector a few hours later. "I managed to ping the tower, got you a general location. While I was at it, I also cracked the security code and got you a log of phone calls - there's a bunch from that same number. And it's the only number either in the log or Contacts." Martin's partner had come in by then and looked to where he was pointing on the city map.

"Hey," he commented, "isn't that where the store is, the one that got broken into?"

"Yes, it is. Maybe his killer is still around? But why would he call when he knows the guy's dead! Okonkwo must have known someone else around here. That's not good – it might mean the NNM have already moved into Montreal without us noticing."

"Which would shed a whole different light on that break-in."

"Yes, but I can't for the life of me see what. We haven't heard a word about a Mayan statue up for sale, and what else could they have been after? They didn't take anything else."

"Except for that knitted thing."

"Crocheted," his partner corrected.

"Whatever. But nothing else was taken."

"Maybe the phone wasn't his?"

Martin looked thoughtful: "That's possible - maybe he took someone's phone, either from the store or some-where else. And maybe whoever is calling is trying to reach the person it was stolen from."

"Could be. But why is it a burner phone?"

"Yeah, and why did no one answer when I called back? What's going on? A break-in, a missing store owner who doesn't exist, a missing and seemingly broken valuable statue, a missing owner of the statue, a dead Nigerian gang-ster, and now an anonymous caller on the Nigerian's phone. Lots of missing parts with nothing obvious to con-nect them."

∞

WHEN HER PHONE RANG shortly after she'd hung up, Nurit grabbed it eagerly and yelled into the mouthpiece, "Hello! Where are you?"

She could hardly hear the answer, a stifled "Hi," but it didn't sound like the man she'd talked to before. Appre-hensive, she asked sharply, "Who is this?" and when the person responded with "It's me," she knew it wasn't him. She was not getting a good feeling about any of this. She disconnected and threw the phone away from her, as if by distancing herself physically from it, she could keep the danger away. More than ever, she wished she could leave. But her parents would be arriving any day now and would find it very strange if she wasn't here. They might even call the police this time and she couldn't risk that.

She resumed pacing. *It's ok*, she reassured herself. *It's a burner phone, they can't trace it to me.* She'd called a number of times after she heard about the break-in, but no one had answered, which made her very anxious. She'd really panicked when she heard about the murder. From what she'd manage to gather without asking directly, only one of them was dead. Where was the other one? Why hadn't he called her? And why wasn't he answering? Had he lost the phone? If so, where was it? Afraid that it could somehow lead to her, as she had phoned it, she'd risked exposure to check out the warehouse and the store, but had found nothing. *And now someone is using it. Who?* She needed to know. Who had it? Obviously someone had picked it up, and she really, really hoped it wasn't the police!

The phone rang again and she buried it under the covers and pillows, to make sure Avi and Noemi wouldn't hear it. They'd left the dining room a while ago and were now in their bedroom at the other end of the apartment, maybe even, if she was lucky, with the TV on so they couldn't hear the phone, which kept ringing. Regaining some ability to think clearly, she unburied the phone and swiped the call away. It stopped ringing. She turned it off so it couldn't be traced.

∞

BELLA HAD BARELY turned the key to unlock the door when the phone started ringing. She rushed to deactivate the alarm and managed to reach it on the fourth ring. "Belles Fleurs," she said breathlessly into the receiver.

"What'd she say? What'd she say?"

Bella sat down, half annoyed and half amused. "Yolly!" she remonstrated, "Give me a chance, I haven't even turned the lights on here!"

"Oh! Is it too early?" Without waiting for an answer to this unimportant consideration, Yolly returned to the attack. "You didn't call me back!"

"I was busy. I do have other things to do!"

"Oh, right. But what did he say? What did she say? What was she looking for? What did she find?"

Bella realized any attempt to divert her cousin would be futile, so she gave in and answered the questions. "I haven't talked to Carl yet. And Nurit said you were mistaken, that it wasn't her." She didn't mention Nurit's surreptitious midnight foray at Mathieu's, she'd no idea what it meant and she didn't want to give the already-overly-imaginative 'detective' any more ammunition.

Yolly was affronted. "I was not mistaken! I know what I saw!"

"Shhh! I can hear you!"

Yolly lowered her decibel level, but repeated more adamantly, "I. Was. Not. Mistaken. I saw her!"

"Well, she says it wasn't her. That's all I know."

"What are we going to do about it?"

"What do you mean?" Bella became wary. Yolly didn't need any encouragement to go off the deep end.

"She's obviously lying. So she has something to hide. How can we find out what it is?"

"Yolly, we can't do anything. And *you* certainly can't. We don't know if she's lying and …."

Yolly interrupted her: "She IS lying!"

"Well, even if she is, there's nothing we can do about it."

"We can tell the police!"

Bella was starting to worry about what her impulsive cousin would do. "No, we CANNOT. You can't accuse people without evidence."

"But I SAW her."

"That's not evidence! It would be your word against hers." She managed to stop herself from adding that an adult's word was more likely to be believed than a child's, as this was likely to trigger a tirade on the unfairness of the world. "And people get very upset when you accuse them falsely. YOU could end up in jail!" She was hoping this threat would discourage Yolly.

Sure enough, there was a pause, then a more subdued voice said, "But what can we do then?"

Bella didn't want to lose the advantage she'd gained, so she said quickly, "Let's think about it for a few days. We don't want to do anything rash. I certainly don't want to end up in jail."

Yolly considered this for a moment. "Okay, I guess. I don't want to go to jail either. My parents wouldn't like that." After another minute of thinking, she jumped back in: "But you could tell Uncle Carl when you give him the evidence!"

Bella promised and Yolly let her get off the phone.

∞

SHE REMEMBERED THE PROMISE Yolly had extorted from her that evening and phoned her brother, who sounded mildly surprised to hear from her. "I was about to call, to let you know I'll be away for a few days next week," he said.

This was part of their post-mother-crisis relationship, where one of them was always the designated first responder in case anything happened to her. Bella was dreading the day when she would have to break down and get a cell phone so she could be contacted. This was one thing she and her siblings had in common: aside from Carl's work requirements, none of them used one, and she, for one, wanted to keep it that way.

"Going anywhere nice?"

"Police training. I'm thinking of applying to become an investigator." He'd made the decision to start the training and see if he liked it. The inspector question had managed to pre-occupy him and he'd not dreamed about Jake for a number of nights. He might go through with the entire training if it worked this well; it was good for his health. He realized his sister was talking and tuned back in.

"Oh good! You can take over responsibility for Yolly-the-detective."

Carl hadn't considered that part of the career move. Did he really want to take on his sometimes too enthusiastic cousin? "What's she done now?"

"She's decided she saw something suspicious and she won't let it go." She told Carl about Yolly's 'evidence' and 'observation.' "I'm a little worried she'll do something stupid. I scared her off for now with the threat of jail, but I'm not sure that'll last."

"I guess I'll take the marijuana, although I'm not sure what I can do with it.... Maybe I should ask a couple of uniforms to go by and scare her off!"

"Maybe ... although it'd probably take the whole force!" They both chuckled at their cousin's indomitability. "But you know, it *is* a little strange."

"What is?"

"Well, first of all, she is amazingly observant and often right. But it's more than that. When Mathieu asked Nurit, she got really mad and then got up in the middle of the night to hide a piece of paper with the word 'Gabriel' on it. Sort of secretively."

"Did he ask her about it?"

"No, he didn't want to admit he was spying on her. He even emptied the garbage to find it."

"It's probably nothing."

"That's what I thought. I certainly didn't tell Yolly about it! But it is strange."

∞

THERE WAS A BRIEFING session that afternoon for the officers going on the training course, and Inspector Martin was there to give an overview of what they could expect. During the coffee break, Carl found himself next to the inspector.

"So, you decided to take my advice," Martin said conversationally as he filled his coffee cup.

"Seemed like a good idea .... How's the case coming?"

Martin shrugged. "It may still be open when you become a detective!"

"I hope not, my sister has a store in the next block."

"Is she scared?"

"No, I don't think so. But she knows the people, so she's concerned for them."

"Well, there's not much news. We can't figure out what the Nigerian was doing here in the first place. We managed to trace him from Toronto, but the police there didn't know about any NNM activity either. These guys are nasty but, up to now, not in North America. And they haven't been into old statues anywhere plus the statue that disappeared hasn't shown up anywhere."

"How was he killed?"

"Looks like he was pushed and then hit his head. But we have no idea who pushed him, or why. Or who was with him in that deserted warehouse. And there's been no more NNM activity here or in Toronto since then. So, if your sister can add anything at all, we'd be very happy to hear it!"

Carl hesitated, then went ahead and told him what Yolly had seen, after preceding and following his account with the caveat that this was an extremely imaginative 11-year-old. The other man was interested, even given the qualification. "I don't know about the pot, but the NNM is definitely into drugs elsewhere. Maybe that's what he was doing there, waiting for a deal to go down. Maybe the break-in and statue were just a sideline to their main activity – that makes more sense. And that's interesting about your cousin seeing a woman – it just so happens that yesterday a woman who wouldn't identify herself called the phone we found with the Nigerian," he said. "We couldn't get her to stay on the phone long enough to trace the call, but it came from somewhere in that vicinity. Maybe I'll go talk to your sister."

When Carl looked unnerved, he grinned. "Don't worry, I won't tell on you…"

Carl was about to say, "That's not what I'm afraid of," when the inspector added, "…or take the word of an 11-year-old as evidence."

The session started again and they went back to their seats.

Week 7

He was so excited about his future that he could hardly contain himself or even sit still. He felt like dancing down the street, shouting his happiness to all the world. Wisely, he satisfied himself with doing this only on the inside; on the outside, he maintained the same expressionless look he had adopted during the years of teasing he had lived through. This opportunity was so wonderful; he had dreamed and hoped, but had not expected it to actually materialize. Not only would he be pursuing studies to create a comfortable life for himself and Nando in the future, but in the meantime he would be free of the continual presence of the neighbour's children and their friends, who still looked for opportunities to make his life a misery.

He would welcome a life where he could fully relax at home. Even if that home was one little room in a student residence, it would be his. Only his. The down side was that his brother would not be there. He was not happy about leaving him alone and unprotected, but they had never picked on Nando. He made Nando promise to let him know if that changed – to contact him the very instant, not to think it would go away or that he could handle it himself. He had more confidence in his own abilities than in his brother's: Nando was too trusting, too ready to think the best of everybody. And, in fact, Nando smiled at his worries, but promised he'd do as requested.

∞

"You're taking this seriously? Did Carl tell you how imaginative she is?" Bella asked the detective, as she handed over Yolly's 'evidence'.

"Don't worry, I'm not going to arrest anyone. I'm just looking into it. I'll send this for fingerprinting and DNA testing, you never know, maybe she's right about someone smoking this while he watched the store. Or maybe he was there for the drugs and not the store at all."

"That must be it! My neighbour thought he saw someone dealing in that alley."

When the Inspector looked interested, she told him how they had succeeded in making their street drug-free and Mathieu's worry that the dealers had now returned.

"Hm, yes, that could be it, maybe this Nigerian gang is moving into Montreal and has started with your street. Maybe Okonkwo, maybe the person who killed him, maybe local associates of this Nigerian gang. So the tests could be helpful. I'll also follow up on her observation about the woman, that might turn out useful as well."

"I don't want to get anyone into trouble," she said worriedly.

"You won't," he assured her. "I'll be discreet."

I really hope I'm doing the right thing. Bella observed gloomily that she'd progressed from neighbourhood gossip to police informer. "I'm sure it was nothing," she said out loud.

"Probably. Most of what we follow up is just that. If so, there's no problem, even if she has a secret that's none of our business. I just want to find out about the Nigerian."

First she made sure he realized that everything she was going to tell him was second-hand, that she hadn't seen anything herself. When he assured her that he understood this, she told him where Yolly had found the marijuana butt. Then she told him about Yolly having watched a woman, who she said was Nurit, apparently searching, first around *objets* and then across the street, then pocketing a small something. She also told him about Nurit's angry reaction and apparently secretive disposal of the 'Gabriel' paper. She even told him about Zelda and Noemi's not knowing anyone or anything of that name.

He wrote everything down carefully, including the names and co-ordinates of all the people involved.

"You won't be getting in touch with Yolly, though, will you?" Bella knew there'd be no stopping her, ever, if she knew the police were following up on the clues she'd provided.

"Not unless it is absolutely necessary."

"I sincerely hope that never happens!"

∞

BACK AT THE STATION, Inspector Martin filled out the paperwork and sent off the marijuana butt for analysis, then sat back and thought about the case. The notebook was starting to fill up – nothing clear, no evidence, but quite a few suspicious people and events. So far he could see no way they were linked to each other or to the NNM. Maybe they weren't, maybe they were all just unlucky at being in the wrong place at the wrong time. But he wouldn't believe that until he had investigated the other possibilities.

Maybe this latest piece would provide a clue. He turned on his computer and searched for links between 'Gabriel' and the NNM gang. Nothing. There were no known members or associates with that name. Was it even a name? Could it be a word? maybe a codename for a planned action? He had his tech wiz add it to the list of parameters he'd assembled for more painstaking searches.

Then he looked up Nurit, but found nothing suspicious. Born in Tel Aviv, living in London for the past five years, the only remotely dubious fact was that she'd continued her studies even though she'd flunked out twice. She'd managed to get into other schools each time. He wondered how she could afford all this education that she didn't seem to be profiting from; he'd looked up her family and seen that they weren't wealthy. Maybe drug-dealing? But he found no indication of this.

Maybe she has a sugar daddy; maybe that's who her secret Gabriel is. He couldn't find any 'Gabriel' connected to her, but that would make sense if their affair was secret, for instance if he was married.

It was only because the weather was so enticing that he followed up right away. The nighttime thunderstorm had reduced the humidity, and the day was hot, dry, and sunny, so he went to pay Nurit a visit. He rang the bell of Noemi and Avi's flat and waited a few minutes. He rang again, just to be sure, and had almost given up when he heard the intercom. "Yes? Who is this?"

"Police. I'm looking for Nurit Azoulay."

The door was buzzed open. When he looked up the stairs, he saw a pregnant woman who could obviously not walk very fast and didn't look happy to have had to answer the door.

"I'm not sure if she's here, I was sleeping," she said accusingly.

He took out his identification card and waved it towards her. "Sorry to disturb you, I'm Police Inspector Stéphane Martin." When her look become anxious, he added hastily, "I just want to have a word with her."

"I'll see if she's in." She didn't invite him up, but didn't close the upstairs door as she turned away. After a few minutes, during which Inspector Martin enjoyed the sunshine and slight breeze, another woman appeared, this one shorter, darker, not pregnant, and no happier to see him.

"Yes?" she said sharply. "You wanted to see me?"

She was obviously not going to ask him up either. He tried to look harmless and casual as he spoke loudly enough for her to hear. "Just following up on a few things."

She interrupted him brusquely, "Things about what?"

He tried to look even more casual, "About the break-in the other week. At the store in your neighbourhood."

"What does that have to do with me? I don't live here!"

"I'm just following up on some information we received. Were you in the vicinity of the store *objets* last," he checked his notebook, "Tuesday around 9:00 a.m.?"

"NO, I was not! it's that stupid snooping girl again, isn't it! I was not there, it wasn't me, how dare she go to the police, how dare she spread these rumours about me. I'll sue her, tell her that. I'll make sure her stupid little ass goes to jail, see how she likes that, I'll ruin her the way she's trying to ruin me, spreading these lies about me!"

When he could get a word in, Inspector Martin tried to stem her tirade, saying mildly, "It wasn't her and I'm just asking questions here. No one's reputation is ruined, no one's going to jail."

"Well, it wasn't me!"

"Okay, okay." He wrote something down in his notebook. "Just one other thing," he spoke quickly as she looked ready to slam the upstairs door. "Is this phone number familiar to you?" He was looking down to read off the number, so he almost missed the look of fear, which was replaced immediately by a totally blank expression.

"Why do you ask me that? What's that got to do with anything?"

"Just following up on some information."

"No," she replied in a flat voice that matched her face.

He decided he might as well continue, once he was there. "Do you know anyone called Gabriel?"

Her reaction was well beyond what he expected: she looked ready to faint as she yelled, "No, no, no! I don't know anything! Leave me alone!" before banging the door shut.

She leaned against the closed door, her pounding heart filled with fear. However had they found out about Gabriel? And traced him to her? First Noemi had asked and now the police. Had he gone to the police? Would he dare? He would be in as much trouble as her. But maybe he preferred prison to the alternative. If so, she was in real trouble and needed to leave immediately. But if he hadn't and the police were just fishing, that would be the worst thing to do. And who had answered her phone call? Was it the police? Or just some random person who had found the phone?

She needed information, she couldn't make any decision unless she knew what she was dealing with. She had only heard bits and pieces of neighbourhood talk, mostly from Mathieu. She needed to speak with someone who really knew what was going on. She had no idea where her contact was and she had no phone number for him. The old number was no longer viable; she was supposed to have received the new number from what had become a dead end; clearly, whoever had the phone now wasn't going to give it to her. Their contingency communication system involved a drop box in London, which was a problem, because she couldn't get it unless she was there physically, in England. She really needed to talk to him, to find out what the hell had happened! Obviously something had gone wrong, but what exactly? And how much trouble was she in?

Her panic was increasing as she ran through the questions in her mind. What about her phone? She'd turned it off immediately the other night, but maybe they could still trace it! She ran to her room, opened the phone and tore out the SIM card. She tried to rip it up; when that only succeeded in breaking a fingernail, she threw it down and stomped on it. Then, for good measure, she stamped on it a few more times until it looked ruined. Still not satisfied, she smashed the phone itself against the floor.

She was panting from the exertion. Suddenly remembering that she was not alone, she held her breath and listened. When she heard nothing, she concluded that her sister-in-law had gone back to rest at the other end of the apartment. She sat down on the bed and tried to think rationally. She really did need to find out what had happened so she could figure out if she was in real trouble or not.

And the only person she could ask was her contact. And the only way she could talk to him was to get the new phone number. Which was only available in London. So she needed to go there. With any luck, she could fly there and back before anyone missed her. She left a note saying 'back soon', rushed downstairs, and grabbed a taxi to the airport.

∞

WOW, HE THOUGHT as he walked back to his car, *that woman does not like to be questioned! And her reaction to the name Gabriel ... if he's her boyfriend, he must be someone really important, someone with lots to lose if his secret comes out.* Martin had found her responses to all his questions interesting, especially her reactions to the phone number and name, so he assigned an officer to watch her. When this officer called him excitedly half an hour later to say she'd just jumped in a cab which he was following and which looked like it was headed to the airport, he found it even more interesting.

It looked like a flight in response to his visit; he just had no idea why. Where was she going? He would very much like to know. Could she be going to Nigeria? The only possible connection he'd found was the phone call to the phone found on the dead Nigerian which had maybe been made by her. If she left the country, he would lose his only possible, albeit slim, clue. But he had no reason to detain her. The only thing he could do was to try to rattle her and see if that produced any results. She'd been pretty upset by his questions, perhaps he could shake her up even more.

He jumped into his own car and used his siren to race to the airport. He left the car in the no parking zone outside the departures area, yelling, "Cop car," to the security guard. The tailing officer had kept him updated on their whereabouts and he'd managed to arrive first, so he was inside the terminal when she got there. He waited until she was at the Air Canada desk buying her ticket before he approached.

"Hello, Ms. Azoulay, are you going somewhere?" he asked in a relaxed tone. He was pleased at her reaction, which was almost as extreme as when he'd mentioned Gabriel.

"Is there any reason why I shouldn't be?" she managed to sputter.

"No reason," he said mildly. "Just asking."

"Are you going to stop me?" She'd recovered enough to become belligerent.

"No," he answered even more mildly, "it's a free country, you can go if you like."

She turned her back on him ostentatiously and, grabbing her ticket and small carry-on bag, literally ran away. He let her go and interrupted the next customer to talk to the ticket agent who'd been serving her.

"Excuse me," he showed his ID card, "police business."

After the customer stepped back, the agent told him Nurit was on the next flight to London. Not what he'd expected. Why was she going to London? He knew that was where she lived, but hadn't a clue why she was going there. Unless it was to see her Gabriel? That was probably it. And nothing to do with his case. But still ... why was she so rattled? If it hadn't been for the phone call, he'd have left her alone. But the woman's voice on the other end could very possibly have been hers. He needed to know if she was the woman who had made the phone call to a member of the notorious NNM gang before he could write her off. And why.

The only innocent explanation he could come up with was that this was the phone she used to communicate with her secret lover and that she'd lost it outside the store *objets*. By coincidence, the Nigerian had, that very night, broken into the store and happened to find her phone and picked it up, before being pushed to his death in the deserted warehouse. It was possible. But in that case, why was there no service for the only phone number listed in its directory: Why wouldn't her Gabriel answer if he thought it was her? And why was that number now out of service? Unless he knew the phone had been lost. And if he did know that, they must have been in touch. So why did she need to fly to London in such a hurry?

Possible... possible enough that she could be completely innocent and uninvolved. But suspicious enough that he was very interested in what she did in London. He couldn't go any official route; he would need some real evidence for that. For the same reason, he couldn't jump on a plane and go himself – he didn't think his boss would approve the expense. But, as it happened, London was one of the places where he had a contact he could ask in an unofficial capacity, someone at Scotland Yard who owed him a favour.

HER ANXIETY HAD SOARED. Worried as she'd been before, she was now so frightened that she only managed to keep going forward by calling on every bit of will and determination she possessed. She had no idea what to do, whether to go or stay. What was he doing in the airport? He must have followed her. She'd been so caught up in fear she hadn't even noticed, which was very bad. Normally, her vigilance was much more fine-tuned and she could immediately spot tail and/or cop within her vicinity. She'd completely missed it this time, he'd taken her by surprise. Unable to think straight, she continued with her plan. He still hadn't arrested her, so maybe he really was still fishing and had no actual evidence. She would have to proceed on that assumption. Otherwise she was in terrible trouble anyway and it wouldn't much matter what she did. Would he let her leave the country?

When he didn't reappear, she boarded the plane and took her seat apprehensively. However, the flight took off without incident and the further away they got, the more she relaxed in her seat. When they reached cruising altitude, she even fell asleep for a few hours.

She disembarked, feeling much calmer, and looking forward to getting some answers and finding out what had happened. She took the tube into the city and made her way to Hyde Park, full of tourists even this early in the morning. She bought a new phone at a kiosk near the park and walked around for a while. When she was sure no one was watching, she sat down on a bench, where she admired the flowers and retrieved the phone number from the piece of paper stuck on its underside.

Inspector Martin's contact had made it to the airport in time to see Nurit arrive. He followed her onto the subway, to the phone kiosk and then to the park, where he saw her furtively retrieve the phone number. He'd had to stay far enough away that he wasn't able to hear any of the phone conversation which followed. He was trying to unobtrusively get a little closer when she turned suddenly and caught his eye before he could turn away. She immediately ended her call, jumped up, and started running away.

He ran after her even though he knew it was useless: she'd spotted him and would notice if he reappeared. He had no backup. He was on his own, doing a personal favour. His boss would go ballistic if he asked for help in following a foreigner on no evidence.

She kept up a jogging pace until she reached the tube station, where she sprinted down the stairs. Working on reflex, she bought a ticket to the most crowded tourist spot she knew. At Covent Garden, she forced herself to walk slowly, strolling around the market, browsing at the stalls.

After fifteen minutes, she'd seen no one remotely interested in her. Maybe she'd imagined the cop … maybe she was just being paranoid … why would a London cop be interested in her? Maybe he wasn't even a cop. But her gut told her differently. Her cop sense had kicked back in. Maybe he was just checking her out as a man though, not as a cop – she would like to believe that.

Surely they didn't have anything on her. That cop in Montreal obviously didn't, or he wouldn't have let her leave the country. And why would the London police be interested in her all of a sudden? She'd been here five years and had never encountered the cops in all that time. Which was the way she liked it. They would not be happy if cops started following her. They were already displeased, as her contact had just made abundantly clear. They blamed the Montreal mess on her. She'd tried to explain about the darkness and Gabriel, but he didn't care and cut her off mid-explanation. If there were any more hiccups, they would stop doing business with her. He hadn't said, but she knew, that they would kill her in an instant if they thought there was even a possibility that she'd lead the cops to them. If the cops were on to her, the best thing would be to evaporate. Totally. Her family would freak but that couldn't be helped. Better missing than dead! After another half hour's browsing with no one interested in her, she was starting to feel better, almost convinced that she'd been mistaken. The opposite was too dreadful to contemplate.

She passed another half hour seated at an outdoor café. Sipping her coffee, she kept a sharp lookout, her head continually swivelling as she tried to keep an eye on all directions. When she saw nothing suspicious, she decided it had been her heightened imagination, stimulated by fear and lack of sleep. She would stay on alert, but there didn't seem to be a need for her to flee, at least not yet. It was probably safe to return to Montreal.

∞

WHEN HER WATER BROKE, Noemi shouted for Nurit, but no one came. When her repeated shouts brought no response, she started getting scared. Was she alone in the apartment? She was having a contraction, she was pretty sure her real labour was starting, birthing time was definitely here. And she was alone! In between the spasms, she dragged herself over to the phone, speed dialed Avi, and started jabbering as soon as he picked up.

Avi, predisposed to panic, was, for the first time in their relationship, the less agitated of the two. He tried really hard to stay unflustered when he realized what his wife was saying, and promised to get there as soon as he could. When he got off the phone, he started panicking about the hour it would take him, even if he could find a taxi right away. He couldn't leave Noemi alone all that time – where the hell was Nurit? This was exactly why she was supposed to be there! He made an effort to stop dwelling on problems and to focus on constructive ideas.

"Ah!" he dialed Belles Fleurs. When Bella answered, he tried to speak calmly and coherently: "Bella, you have to go over to see Noemi, she is starting labour and it will take me an hour to get there." As his calmness began to crack , his speed increased: "I called you because I knew I'd find you. Nurit's not there. She should be, but she isn't. Can you go over there? Please, she's all alone, Noemi, she's all alone and scared. Please." As soon as Bella said "Yes," he went running to find a taxi.

Despite his efforts at composure, his urgency had communicated itself. Bella was alone in the store, and stood for a moment, unable to move. Then she ran around like a madwoman for another minute searching for the pad of

paper and pen sitting right in front of her. She scribbled
BABY on a sheet of paper, which she stuck on the door.
She remembered to lock the door, had to run back in to
set the alarm, almost forgot to lock the door the second
time, then went running towards Noemi's house, imagining she could hear the labour groans three blocks away. She
had no idea what to do when someone was in labour but
at least she could be present. And call a taxi. Or an ambulance! Hopefully Noemi would know which one was
needed.

Bella didn't stop running until she'd reached the first
floor landing. She rang the bell and peered through the
door to see if anyone was there. She could just see the first
few stairs leading up to the top floor where they lived. She
rang the bell again and, when no one came, started pounding on the door, yelling that it was her, Bella, she was there
for Noemi. Then she realized that all that pounding might
scare her, and even, god forbid, make the baby think twice
about emerging into this noisy world! She breathed in and
out, trying to quell her panic, which wouldn't help anyone.
She waited another minute, then called out as loudly (and
calmly) as she could, "Noemi? It's Bella. I've come to help
you." She put her ear to the door and heard footsteps getting louder. "I'm coming," she heard, followed by a click
as the lock was released, "It's open now."

Bella hurried up the stairs, where she found Noemi between contractions and coherent. When Bella babbled that
she didn't know what to do, Noemi said they should call a
cab, that it wasn't urgent enough to require an ambulance.
Bella tried to match Noemi's unruffled demeanor; just
knowing that she was not alone had allowed the mother-
to-be to stop panicking. Bella picked up the bag that Noemi had packed two weeks before and they went downstairs to wait for the taxi. Noemi had to sit on the bottom

step when she was hit with another contraction, and managed to moan instead of scream. When the contraction passed, Bella made conversation to distract her. She wasn't very good at prattling, she tried to think of what Mathieu would talk about, but couldn't think of anything. Out of desperation, she asked about Nurit.

The distraction was successful, perhaps because Noemi was so annoyed with her sister-in-law. "She was supposed to be here with me. So I wouldn't be alone. But after the cop came, no more Nurit! She left a note saying *'back soon'*, and that was that." She paused a moment, in anticipation of more pain, but the contraction backed off. "She's been weird anyway, even more so than usual, these last few days, ever since I asked her about Gabriel."

"Does she know a Gabriel?" Bella asked.

"She said no. Avi thought he remembered that she'd known an African Gabriel in England, that she'd even been dating him. But she said no, that wasn't his name. Then she stomped off to her bedroom and I haven't really seen her since, except to tell her when the officer came."

At the mention of the police officer showing up to question Nurit, Bella felt a stab of guilt, suspecting that she'd been the cause of Nurit's flight and Noemi's distress. The taxi arrived just then, so she was saved from having to confess.

When they got to the hospital, Noemi was whisked away by efficient nurses. Bella waited outside, using Noemi's phone to let Avi know they'd arrived safely.

"Thank you, thank you so much, thank you. I'm stuck here, on the bridge, nothing's moving, I can't see why, and the cabbie doesn't know anything either. He's been on the radio to the dispatcher, they don't know what the holdup is. I don't know how long I'll be."

"That's okay." Now that Avi was back in his familiar flapped state, Bella found herself calming down in reaction. "It doesn't seem urgent, she's not about to have the baby. I think you have lots of time."

"Good, oh so good. Can you wait with her? Until I get there? I don't want her to be alone. Nurit was supposed to be with her but I can't find her. Will you stay?"

"Yes of course, no problem. I'll be here until you come."

"Thank you! My parents are on their way, they left yesterday, I guess they're somewhere in the air now, but I can't call them."

"That's okay," again Bella found herself trying to talk him down, "they said you have lots of time."

"Okay, okay, thank you. What else do I have to do? I can't think…."

Bella realized it would be up to her to end the conversation. When she spotted the nurse coming towards her, she said, "The nurse is here, gotta go," and hung up.

∞

MATHIEU DIDN'T KNOW whether he was feeling worried, angry, or sad. He didn't even know which one he *should* be feeling. Not only had they not indulged in the romantic dinner he'd envisioned, he hadn't seen or heard from Nurit since he'd found that scrap of paper. She hadn't shown up that evening, which was unusual in itself. They hadn't made definite plans, but it had become their routine to have dinner and then spend the evening and night together. But last night, there'd been no sign of her, no phone message either and, when he'd called, her phone went to voicemail. Since then, he'd been calling regularly, but her number had stopped accepting messages and was now out of service . He knew she'd pulled vanishing acts before, it seemed to be her modus operandi. He was hurt that she'd done it again; he'd thought they really clicked, but maybe he was wrong. Or maybe they just hadn't known each other long enough yet for her to change her habits.

He looked at the purring cat on his lap. "You don't miss her at all, do you, Fritz?" His house-mate half-opened one eye, his half-asleep version of nodding in agreement, then closed it again and went back into a deep sleep. "At least we have each other," Mathieu sighed, trying to remember an apt quote from one of his favourite movies: *We'll always have Paris? This is the beginning of a beautiful friendship?* But none really fit this occasion.

He sighed again at his unsuccessful effort to distract himself from the inglorious collapse of yet another relationship. He found himself almost hoping something had happened to her, so he could just be worried and throw himself into saving her. *How likely is that?* he chided himself. *And what kind of person does that make me?*

He was almost depressed enough to dig out the phone number for his grandmother's neighbour's cousin's friend, or whoever she was; almost … but not quite. He had called in sick that morning, unable to face the world. Now he felt like that was exactly what he needed: activity, life, stimulation, things happening, distractions.

"Enough of this sitting around feeling sorry for ourselves," he scolded his profoundly content cat and stood up, eliciting a growl from Fritz, who found himself unceremoniously dumped on the floor. Mathieu glanced down briefly. "Hang around if you like. *I'm* going out!"

Once outside, he headed for his usual first stop. When he got to Belles Fleurs, he pushed at the door absently. When it didn't budge, he pushed again, thinking it must have gotten warped with the humidity. When that had no effect, he emerged from his personal funk long enough to look at his phone and confirm it wasn't closing time yet. When he peered through the door, it looked dark. Finally, he refocused and found himself looking at a piece of paper taped to the door, with the word 'BABY' written in large capital letters.

When the words had sunk in, his self-absorption vaporized and he leaped into his usual attitude of concern for others. "Mon dieu, mon dieu!! It must be Noemi!"

Even while he wondered why Noemi's baby had caused Bella to close her store, he was already hurrying over there. Maybe there was something he could do. He liked helping people, it had become his role in the neighbourhood. People called him when they needed to know what was happening, or when they needed help. If he couldn't personally do it, he usually managed to find someone who could.

"Mathieu to the rescue!" he laughed at himself as he hurried. When he got there, he ran up to the first landing, just as Bella had done a few hours earlier. There was no answer to his bell ringing or door pounding; his phone call went to voicemail.

In the anticlimax that followed this surge of adrenalin, Mathieu remembered that this was also Nurit's home, at least in Montreal. The fact that she hadn't answered the door either brought back his earlier worry/anger/sadness. Disgusted with himself for reverting to self-pity, he decided to go home and lose himself in his online gaming community and avatar; a fantasy personality seemed more likely to be satisfying today than the flesh and blood one.

∞

ZELDA WAS ON her way to *objets* when she saw the BABY sign at Belles Fleurs. She was late, much later than she'd meant to be. She knew she needed to be open at regular hours if she wanted people to come and buy things. That was the kind of thing Daniel had been good at, and she was not.

She'd intended to be there in the morning. She'd set her alarm and gotten up after just a few extra snoozes. She was making breakfast when the ringtone on her phone announced a text message. She wasn't much of a texter, had only gotten the phone because it seemed a business necessity. The only person who texted her with any regularity was Daniel, and she hadn't received a word from him since the night of the break-in . When she recognized the unfamiliar sound, she ran for the phone, which she found at the bottom of her bag.

The message was from an unfamiliar number: "Hey Aunt Zelda, this is Peter, Daniel says hi."

She was bewildered. The only Peter she could think of who could be calling her Aunt was her sister's grandson, the one in Winnipeg, whose Bar Mitzvah she'd attended last year. But why would he have her number? Had he gotten it from Daniel? How could he know Daniel? Was Daniel in Winnipeg? Was this actually from Peter, or from Daniel pretending to be Peter? Did he know about Peter? Was it a coded message that he thought she'd understand, something to do with Winnipeg and her sister? Or was it a straightforward message just to tell her not to worry about him, that he was okay?

What should she do? Should she do anything? Was this Daniel's way of telling her not to look for him? Or was it the opposite? Should she call her sister? But chances were Peter hadn't mentioned this to Nelly. If he had, Nelly would most probably have been on the phone to her already. Should she call Peter? But what would she say? She didn't want to scare him or get him thinking this was more than a friend of hers running into him. If Daniel was in danger, the last thing she wanted was to point to him. And if the message hadn't even come from Peter, what would he make of her call?

She appreciated the text, though. At least it told her that Daniel was alive (she'd been so scared he was dead!) and, maybe, for some reason, had been in Winnipeg. Finally, not knowing what else to do, she sent a reply: "Thanks! Love, Zelda." At least this would tell whoever had sent the text, Peter or Daniel, that she'd received it. And, if there was anything more to be said, he could say it…. The phone, however, stayed stubbornly silent.

By this time, of course, she was late.

So here she was, hurrying to the store. She wondered if she should tell Bella about the text. She hadn't known the other woman long, but felt a connection with her, probably because of the yarmulka. But she was afraid it was better to say nothing; she really didn't know what was going on and didn't want to endanger Daniel, Bella, or even Peter, through her actions.

A better idea would be to convene the coven again. Perhaps it was their magic that had resulted in the text; maybe it could bring forth another, more comprehensible, one. She would summon the messenger of the universe and make that request.

This was as far as she'd gotten in her thinking when she reached the flower shop. She was going to just pass by with a wave to Bella when she saw the 'BABY' note on the door. The midwife in her surfaced. Forgetting all about Daniel, she pulled out the phone again and left messages for both Bella and Noemi, offering her help in any baby-related capacity.

∞

WHEN BELLA LEFT the hospital, Noemi had already been in labour for eight hours and the nurse said it didn't look like the baby would be born anytime soon. Avi had arrived and his parents had come directly from the airport. Avi had spent the time in the birthing room and Bella had waited in the family room with his parents. She offered to take them to Avi's home, but they said they would wait at the hospital. They were indeed old and frail, she could see why Avi and Nurit didn't want to upset them too much. They kept asking about Nurit, but she had nothing to tell them. She had no idea where their daughter was. Even though Noemi had told her that they'd gotten used to Nurit's vanishing acts, they were visibly shocked that she would not be there for the birth of the first grandchild in the family.

When she got off the bus, it was already past midnight. She arrived home beat, too wired to sleep and, since the hospital food had not looked appetizing enough for her to eat much, starving. She made herself a sandwich and settled down to watch some mindless TV, then noticed her voicemail light flashing.

Might as well listen to my messages. I'm not sleepy anyway. She heard Mathieu's and Zelda's offers to help, but figured she would call both of them the next day as it was already so late; she hadn't seen any lights on downstairs. There were yet more messages, making Bella feel like she'd been away for weeks instead of hours. Yolly wanted to know if there was any news and if Nurit had finally admitted that she, Yolly, had been right.

The last call was from her sister, wanting to schedule another family dinner for when both Carl and Lila would be back in town. "Maybe I should be the one away next time," she grumbled, more from habit than actual unwillingness. Over the past year or so, her family had shed the toxic dynamic she'd grown up with, the result of her mother becoming frailer and, perhaps as well, of her rigid grandfather's passing. The permanent bitterness surrounding her mother, sister, and cousin had subsided, and, as a result, her brother had loosened up, especially around Lila's girls. Eddie was much more likeable in his post-alcoholic persona, George as uncommunicative as ever but less iciness emanated from him. And maybe she herself was no longer quite so determined to hold them all at longer-than-arm's length. With all these individual changes, they'd become a little closer, and there had even been moments of warmth. She knew she'd say yes to the dinner.

She watched TV until she found herself nodding off during a noisy action-filled car chase, at which point she dragged herself to bed.

∞

NOEMI'S LABOUR lasted 24 hours. Finally, exhausted beyond anything she'd ever imagined, she gave a last shove and out he came. Her fatigue evaporated for an instant, enough for her to clasp the baby to her breast before collapsing.

Avi was beside himself. He'd been at her side for most of the time and had managed to subdue his panic and worrying for once, helping his wife breathe, push, and relax. Now, holding his newborn son, his joy was boundless, he felt like he would drown in it, he'd never felt so happy in his life.

He brought his parents to the newborns' viewing window and proudly pointed to his baby. His son. Their grandson. They glowed with almost as much pride as he felt.

"Now I can take you home," he said to them. "You must be worn out ."

"Yes," said his mother. "But we wanted so much to see him."

Avi nodded with complete understanding. "I'll take you now," he said. "You can rest and I'll bring you back later. Noemi will be awake then."

His mother started to gather up their belongings, which had spread out during the 20 hours they'd been there. "Where is Nurit?" she asked her son. "Do you know where she is?"

Avi hadn't thought of his sister at all during the last few hours, he shook his head. "Isn't that just like her," he said, "to not be around, just when we could have used her. She never thinks of anyone but herself!"

His mother started to defend her, but Avi was too tired to care. "I had to call Bella," he said, "because Nurit left Noemi all alone. She was supposed to be there. To help."

"Maybe something happened to her?" his mother said worriedly.

"Hah! Maybe!" he snorted, in a skeptical voice. They'd had this discussion before: his mother worried, his father trying to think the best about his daughter, Avi believing they were both being blind.

∞

BELLA RETURNED BRIEFLY to the hospital that afternoon. She wasn't exactly a baby-lover, but she'd been involved enough in this baby's arrival that she wanted to see the flesh and blood result. She'd called Zelda and Mathieu to let them know about the birth. She'd been dismayed by Mathieu's mood; after spending a few frustrating minutes trying to cheer him out of his funk, she'd suggested he come with her to see the newborn. But he'd declined, saying he preferred the company of his online buddies. Still preoccupied by her neighbour's uncharacteristic depression, she forgot to go to Belles Fleurs to pick something up for the new mother and baby and had to settle for a tiny teddy bear from the gift shop. She found Noemi alone and dozing. Her eyes opened when Bella put the bear on the table, and she struggled to sit up.

"Don't," Bella said very softly. "I was just leaving this for you."

"Thanks," Noemi's eyes started to close again, then she added, "I forgot a few things at home, mostly the skin cream and lip guck, my mouth is so very dry. Oh, and my slippers. Avi's already left. Could you get them for me?"

"Yes of course. Where are they?"

By the time she finished telling Bella where to find everything, Noemi's eyes had closed again. Before leaving the floor, Bella got the nurse to show her which one of the indistinguishable bundles was Baby Azoulay. She waved enthusiastically at the unresponsive infant, then left to do her errand.

She had just stepped off the elevator when she found her way blocked by Pedro. "Bellísima, I hope you're not sick!?"

She had to laugh at his woebegone expression. "No, no, it's a happy thing. Noemi had her baby."

His crestfallen face changed instantly into a smile. "Oh, that is indeed a happy thing. She is well? The baby too?"

"Yes, everyone is fine, and I think she's very happy to have it out!" Bella, also happy to have the birth and pregnancy over with, included Pedro in her general feeling of well-being. *Maybe he's not so bad, he seems to care about Noemi.*

"Maybe I will go see her, do you think she would like that?"

"Maybe. She was sleeping when I left just now, but maybe when she wakes up."

He nodded. "I will do that."

"But what are you doing here? Are you okay?"

"My grandmother is here."

She looked at him with concern. "Your grandmother? She's in the hospital?"

He nodded. "She had a thing, a heart thing, so they are keeping her here for observation."

"I'm so sorry." She didn't know what else to say. She didn't know anything about his family.

"I'm just on my way to see her."

"I hope it turns out to be nothing serious."

"Thank you, Bellísima." For the first time, she found his use of that name endearing rather than irritating.

∞

INSPECTOR MARTIN was just starting his shift when he received the email. His contact in London hadn't been able to continue following after the incident in the park when he'd seen Nurit pick up the phone and number. Besides the fact that she'd noticed him, he'd had a work call to look into an emergency. However, he had put out an APB with her name and had just gotten a hit: she'd booked a flight to Montreal.

The information from London had increased his suspicions. The first thing she'd done was get a new phone, retrieve a phone number from a public park bench, and make a phone call. Even if she had a secret boyfriend, this was strange behaviour. It was looking more and more like his suspicions were founded. Maybe the little girl was right and it was about drugs, maybe she was connected to the NNM, maybe Gabriel was her connection in London. He decided to increase the pressure on her, see if that produced any results. So he was at the airport, this time with his partner, when she landed.

"Welcome back, Ms. Azoulay," he said pleasantly, "that was a short trip."

"What do you want?"

"I was wondering if you would like to assist our investigation by answering a few questions."

"I've already told you, I don't know anything about any of this."

"Yes I know that's what you said, but I was wondering if you had reconsidered, if you would like to tell us about your connection with the NNM?"

"The what?"

"The New Nigerian Movement."

"I've never hear of it."

"Are you sure?"

"Of course I'm sure!"

"Just checking that you're sure you don't know them."

"I told you, I don't! Do I need a lawyer?"

"That is up to you. Do you need a lawyer?"

"Am I under arrest?"

"No, not at this moment. But we would be grateful if you would answer a few questions."

"Do I have to?"

"No."

"Can I go?"

"Yes, but the next time I see you, it may be to arrest you for murder."

Murder?

They watched her stagger away. His partner said, "We don't have her for murder! You don't really think she killed him, do you?"

"No," Inspector Martin replied, "but I'm sure she knows something about it. Let's make sure we keep an eye on her. And better if she knows it. I'm guessing she's the type to get more and more rattled. Maybe she'll crack."

∞

NURIT WAS TRYING to think her way out of this mess.

Murder!

Obviously they had no proof or they would have arrested her right there. If they dug deep enough, was it possible they could uncover her connection to the NNM? They seemed to know about it already. How? She'd covered her tracks at each step, but maybe not well enough, not in anticipation of a murder investigation!

She needed somewhere to hide so she could think this through clearly, but her family would be wondering where she was by now. For all she knew, her parents were here already. Oh god – maybe the baby had already been born! How was she going to explain this? She needed time to think but wasn't sure she could afford it. She also couldn't meet her family in this state. No matter what she said, they'd know something was wrong.

She spotted a café sitting conveniently in her path. She bought a coffee and sat down at the darkest most out-of-the-way table. Taking a deep breath, she thought, *Okay*. She was aware of the minutes ticking away as she sat there trying to figure out her future. So far, she'd failed to come up with any feasible plan. She was running out of options along with time. She took a sip of coffee and tried to keep her mind from jumping all over the place.

She decided to concentrate on the immediate future: one day at a time. She finished the coffee , went and got another one, and sat down to figure out her next step. Should she call her brother or just show up? They were used to her unpredictability, with any luck she wouldn't even have to explain. And if she was not in luck? Well, she would deal with that when it arose, her brain felt that it would explode with trying to figure things out. She finished the second coffee. Trying to muster a scrap of enthusiasm, she went to find the bus that would take her into the city.

As soon as she walked into Avi's apartment, she knew she was out of luck: her parent's suitcases sat in the middle of the living room. At least no one was home. Although that probably meant the baby had at long last made its entrance, without her there to help as she'd been supposed to. At least it gave her another few minutes to compose herself and try to think of a plausible explanation. She was generally a good liar, but this situation was straining her abilities.

She'd have to bluster her way through, without offering any explanations. It had worked before. She turned on the phone actually registered in her name, which had been turned off since she'd left for London, and called Avi. It went to voicemail. *Okay… let's try Noemi.* That number had no service. Her parents were probably the only people in Israel without cell phones and their landline was back in Tel Aviv. She called Avi again and left a breezy message: "Hi bro, it's your sister, wondering where you are."

When she sat down, her exhaustion caught up with her. The few hours' sleep she'd managed to grab on each flight didn't add up to even one decent night's worth. She considered her situation: no one was here, she didn't really know where they were, she'd left a message, and eventually, they would find her; a nap was what she most needed. With that, she went to her room and was asleep almost instantly.

She was wakened by the sound of movement in the living room. She opened the bedroom door and found herself, still half asleep, looking into Bella's equally surprised face. Nurit found her tongue first.

"Oh hi," she said in the same breezy voice she'd used for Avi's message. "What's up? Where is everyone?"

Bella bit back her first reaction. It really wasn't any of her business where Nurit had been, even though she, Bella, had had to come running to make up for her absence! In any case, she knew enough about dysfunctional family dynamics to really not want to get involved in someone else's. So she said mildly, "They're at the hospital, Noemi asked me to pick up a few things for her."

"Oh!" exclaimed Nurit disingenuously, widening her eyes. "Did she have the baby already?"

Bella again swallowed her reproach and said, even more mildly, "Yes, yesterday."

"Oh how lovely!" Nurit injected enthusiasm into her breeziness. "Everything went okay?"

"She was in labour for 24 hours." Bella couldn't quite keep the sarcasm out of her voice, but Nurit seemed oblivious to Bella's mood: "Oh yeah, but everyone is okay?"

"Yes, they're fine." And then, because she couldn't restrain herself, she asked, "Don't you want to see them?"

"Yes, of course I do! Where are they?"

Bella gave her directions on how to get to the hospital and the room number. Nurit was already turning away, when Bella asked, "Do you want to take Noemi the things she wanted?"

"Yes of course!" Nurit turned back. "Do you have a list?"

As she left the apartment, Bella wondered if Nurit was on drugs. She'd seemed so spacey, so not-all-there. Maybe that was her secret, why she disappeared periodically. She'd better check that Nurit really did get to the hospital, so she called Noemi to say Nurit would be bringing her stuff. It was Avi who answered the hospital phone.

"Hi Avi, it's Bella, everything okay?"

"Yes, yes, yes. Noemi and the baby are sleeping, both are beautiful. And tired."

"Great. I won't keep you, I just wanted to tell you I went by your apartment to get some stuff for Noemi, and Nurit was there."

He interrupted sharply: "She was? She's back?"

"Yes, she was there so I told her where you were and she said she'd come to the hospital and bring Noemi's stuff." No need to mention Nurit's spaciness; he'd either see it himself or she'd have recovered by the time she got there. In any case, she told herself firmly once again, it was none of her business.

"Did you tell her my parents are here? And about the baby?"

" I told her about the baby. I didn't mention your parents, but their suitcases are in the living room, so she probably knows."

"Okay, okay, thank you. Why didn't she call me? Where's she been? I don't understand!"

"I don't know, but hopefully you'll see her soon." Bella really wanted to get out from the middle. "If you need anything else, just call, okay? Say hi to Noemi for me." And she got off the phone.

∞

WHEN NURIT GOT to the hospital, she could see that her family was expecting her. *That bitch must have called Avi*, she thought resentfully. *As if it's any of her business*! She pasted on her cheeriest smile and rushed up to her brother, enfolding him in an embrace, "Congratulations, mazel tov!" Turning to her parents, she hugged and kissed them both, keeping up her congratulatory patter.

She smirked inwardly at her success when they all started talking at once:

"Thank you, thank you."

"Nurit where were you?"

"Sweet daughter, we were worried about you!" This last from her father, who she could usually count on to take her side.

"Whoa, slow down," she giggled. "Where's Noemi? Can I see the baby? Where is he?" She started towards the room where her sister-in-law lay, the others following in her wake. She oohed and aahed over the baby, heard details of the birth, and went off to get coffee for her parents and brother, all without having answered any questions about herself.

It wasn't until they were back at Avi's apartment that evening, everyone installed for the night (their parents in Avi and Noemi's room and Avi himself on the living room sofa) that her mother sat her down and said seriously, "Nurit, what is going on? Where were you?"

Years of lying to her mother had honed her skill. During the day she'd had more time to think and had figured out that the best approach was to rely on her mother's desire for her to meet a man and settle down. So she sighed and looked downcast, then said, "You know that guy I was seeing? The one who wasn't ready to commit?" She'd invented this man to deal with previous inquiries. When her mother nodded, she continued, "He was in Toronto, so I went to see him."

"Why couldn't he come here?"

"He didn't have time, he was there on business, just for the one day."

"He came all this way for one day?" Her previous stories had situated this fictional man in London.

"Yes, he was on his way to Chicago. And I haven't seen him for so long and he missed me, so I thought it would be okay if I went just for the day."

"Why didn't you tell Noemi where you were going?"

"I just got so excited when he called, I forgot!" She played up the scatterbrain persona she'd invented in her teens.

"Why was your phone turned off?"

"I forgot to take it!"

She could see her mother's doubts, but it was the best she could do under the circumstances. The bright smile she plastered on deflected further probing.

∞

UNFORTUNATELY, NOEMI wasn't as easy to dupe. Besides being less easily fooled by Nurit in general, she was seriously annoyed about her absence this time. "Where were you!?!" she yelled at her sister-in-law. "You were supposed to be there. To help me, in case Avi wasn't home! What happened?" She finished and sat there, glaring at Nurit, demanding an answer.

Nurit stuck her breezy smile back on and launched into her excuse patter, the one she'd given her mother, about the man she was seeing and the one day in Toronto. She managed to keep going, despite the accusing glare; she finished her spiel without faltering and adopted what she hoped looked like a lascivious leer.

"I'm so sorry, really I am, Noemi, I just didn't think. You know how it is! When love calls?"

At this point, she didn't care if her family believed she was an idiot, just as long as they didn't suspect anything worse. Noemi, for one, seemed to be buying the idiot act. "Well, we certainly won't be depending on you in the future!"

"I'm sorry, I really am, how can I make it up to you?" Nurit considered groveling, then ruled that out as probably counterproductive. "I'll babysit forever. And ever." Noemi was not placated and waved her away. *Oh well,* Nurit shrugged mentally, *I tried. If Noemi wants to stay mad, that's her problem.* She was probably burning too many bridges, getting too many people mad at her, but she couldn't think what else to do.

When she went to smoke her next cigarette outside of the 8-foot no-smoking zone encircling the hospital, she saw the woman standing by the door. She was sure it was the same one she'd seen that morning when they'd left the apartment, and who'd also been here the last time she'd come out to smoke. She smiled at her, just in case it was coincidence, but the other stared back without changing her expression. *Maybe she's not really following me. Maybe she's also visiting someone here,* Nurit hoped, trying to convince herself. But, even if she *was* following her, it wasn't obvious who she was doing it for; it could just as easily be the NNM as the police.

She'd managed to suppress her terror during the past 24 hours as she focused on her family problems. But, of course, it was still there. And her options remained as limited as they'd been the day before. She wasn't sure how long she could continue in this vein, how long she had before it all blew up in her face. If she was going to make her own decision instead of one being forced on her, she needed to act. Sooner rather than later. But she still didn't know what to do. She ground out her cigarette with her heel and went back inside, keeping her eyes firmly forward.

∞

INSPECTOR MARTIN NODDED as he got off the phone and made a note in the file open in front of him. "She noticed the tail at the hospital," he said to his partner. "Let's step it up a notch." Although they had other cases to work on, his boss had been interested in a possible connection to a notorious Nigerian gang moving into their territory. So interested that she'd approved them spending some time and effort on this one, but not much; her continued support depended on results.

Nurit was their most interesting lead at the moment. So the two inspectors dropped in at the hospital for a surprise visit. They weren't disappointed. When she saw them approaching the family room where she sat with her parents, Nurit's face turned white and she got up hastily. After murmuring something, she pulled out her cigarettes and hurried towards the exit. The two officers reached her just as she lit up in the smoking zone.

"What do you want?" she asked aggressively. "Why are you following me?"

"We're not following you," said Martin. "Just wanted to ask if you had anything new to tell us."

"NO!" she yelled loud enough to attract the attention of the other smokers, who turned to watch the drama.

"No," she said more quietly. "I told you, I don't know anything!"

"Okay, just checking to see if anything new had occurred to you."

"NO!" Her raised voice got the attention of the smokers again, and she lowered it with obvious difficulty. "I told you, this has nothing at all to do with me, and there is nothing that can change that. Would you please now leave me alone!"

"As long as you're sure," he continued in the slow plodding voice that he hoped was most likely to infuriate her.

She glared at him, then threw her cigarette on the ground and stomped on it. As she turned to go, he called after her, "Mademoiselle Azoulay!"

"What is it now?" She pivoted back.

He pointed at the butt on the ground. "It's against the law to litter."

"Oh for god's sake!" She picked up the butt and put it into the receptacle indicated, then deliberately turned her back on him and returned to her family.

∞

"There is definitely something going on here. I have no idea if it's related to our dead Nigerian, but we need to find out. Let's keep pushing," Martin remarked to his partner.

"Did you ever follow up with the boy who got knifed?" His partner had been busy on other cases, but Martin had kept him filled in on this one.

"No – I got busy and forgot. You're right. Here we are at the hospital, let's go see if he's still here."

"Do you have the picture with you? of the Nigerian?"

Martin checked his pocket. "Yeah, I do. Let's see if he recognizes it."

Sébastien was still there but dressed and sitting up in the guest chair, waiting to be discharged. He looked up eagerly as the police officers entered, then scowled. "I'm waiting for my mother," he said defiantly.

"Okay, this will just take a minute. I want to show you a picture, see if you recognize him."

Sébastien peered at the photo. "Is this the guy who knifed me?"

"I don't know. Do you recognize him?"

The boy shook his head. "But I told you, I didn't see him at all. Couldn't even tell you if he was white or black."

Martin wanted to make sure he had checked out all possibilities. "Is this maybe the guy who sold you the weed?"

"Oh no! That was a girl!"

Martin hadn't expected this. "It was a girl?" he asked dubiously.

Sébastien nodded. "Yah, well, you know, a woman."

They heard movement in the hall and Sébastien looked anxious again. "You won't tell my mother about any of this?"

"I don't think so. But I may be in touch again."

Back in their car, the officers mulled over this latest development. "Her drug connection is looking more and more probable."

Martin answered, "Maybe ... but would they send this Okwonko guy all the way from Nigeria to sell dime bags of weed? And what about the break-in? the Mayan statue? the death? What does she have to do with all that? And if nothing, then what's she hiding? What was she doing in London? We have to up the pressure on her, see what she knows, see if it's connected to any of this."

"What about that officer whose sister knows her? Can we use that connection?"

Carl had returned from the inspector-training workshop. He'd found it interesting and was thinking that this would be a good step, not only to keep him from thinking about Jake, but because he would enjoy the challenge. So at first he was pleased when Martin came looking for his help. But when he realized what the help entailed, his enthusiasm waned. "You want me to get my sister involved in this?"

"Just peripherally. We don't really know anything, we only have suspicions. So you can't tell her anything, because we don't actually know anything. Be careful what you say," cautioned the inspector. "There's no evidence tying the Azoulay woman to this gang or to the murder. Not even circumstantial, nothing very clear. So we can't spread rumours. Just maybe tell your sister that we're interested in the woman, that the lead we got from her before was very useful. We don't really have anything more than that."

Carl knew this would be a good career move for him. Helping the inspectors solve a homicide, especially one that involved gangs moving into their territory, would give him a leg up in a competitive field. So, even while he was reluctant to involve his family in what could be dangerous, he agreed to do it. But carefully.

He dropped in at Belles Fleurs that afternoon. When he saw the police uniform, Raoul shifted the phone, said "Could you hold on just a moment?" into the receiver and looked at Carl inquiringly.

"I'm looking for Bella?"

Raoul pointed to the café next door. Carl nodded his thanks and left, without offering an explanation to the curious assistant. He found his sister sitting at a table by the counter, reading a newspaper and eating a sandwich. He sat down next to her and said "Hi." She did a double take when she saw him.

"Hi ...," she said doubtfully, then with a little more anxiety, "Is everything okay?"

"Yes, yes," he reassured her, "just stopped by to say hi."

She was staring at him so skeptically that he blushed. "Well, sort of just to say hi," he granted, squirming under her scrutiny.

"What's up? Are you alright?"

"Oh yes, I'm fine, nothing to worry about." This was harder than he'd realized. How could he possibly introduce the subject offhandedly? It wasn't as if they had this sort of conversation on a regular basis. "It's kind of delicate," he began.

When he stopped short, not knowing how to continue, she burst out, "Do you have AIDS?"

"No, no!" – it had never occurred to him that she would worry about something like that – "It's nothing to do with me!"

"Is someone else sick?" He could see she was getting agitated.

"No, no, it's nothing like that. It's work related."

She relaxed visibly, then her anxious look returned. "You mean police business?"

"Yes, but it's nothing." She looked totally unconvinced. "At least nothing serious. Not for you. Or me."

"What *is* it then?"

To hell with subtlety. He could think of no way to say this except to come right out with it. "It's about that woman, the one Yolly saw."

"Nurit?" Bella had almost forgotten having spoken to Carl about this, with all the excitement since.

"She may be involved in something serious."

"Like what?"

"I can't go into details," and, realizing how lame that sounded, he added, "because there's no proof, no evidence, just suspicions. But we're watching her."

"And this is connected to the break-in?"

"And murder."

"This is serious, then!"

"Not that we think she did the break-in or murder or anything."

"So what *do* you think?"

"We think she might know who did do it."

"And that would be?"

"I can't tell you that. But no one you would want to know."

Bella was trying to digest all this – she'd given up on her sandwich, which lay on the discarded newspaper. "Why are you telling me this?"

"Well, I, that is, we, that is, the inspector, would like you to increase the pressure on her. But subtly, just a look, nothing more, nothing so she thinks you actually know anything. I don't want you to do anything dangerous. Please Bella promise me you won't do anything dangerous. Oh god, I shouldn't be doing this, I should have said no, I shouldn't be asking you. Forget I said anything, please just forget it."

Bella watched her brother work himself up into a more agitated state than she'd ever seen. She said slowly, "You want me to help you get evidence against her?"

"No! Definitely not! I don't want you to do anything remotely dangerous. And these are dangerous people. I should never have agreed to do this."

"What do you want then?" Bella couldn't figure out what he was asking.

"They think she's close to cracking. They've got someone watching her and she's getting rattled. They think if there's more pressure, like maybe people she knows giving her suspicious looks, then she'll crack. And confess."

"Really? To what? And how likely is that anyway?"

"I don't know," he admitted. "I've never even seen her. But Inspector Martin has a good reputation."

"What does this even have to do with Zelda's store and the yarmulka?"

"I have no idea. And I really, really don't want you to do anything dangerous. Maybe it's best if you just don't do it and we'll forget I asked. I'll just say no to Martin."

"Well, she is definitely weird," said Bella and she told him about Nurit's disappearance and how spaced out she'd been when she resurfaced. "If you really think she's mixed up in something dangerous, poor Noemi and Avi! And that little baby! I wouldn't want anything to happen to them."

"If it is drugs, as you thought, this would get her into rehab."

"That's true," Bella brightened up. "Okay, I'll do it."

"Are you sure?" Carl wasn't happy with putting his sister at risk.

"No, I mean yes. You're right. If she's innocent, then there's no problem. And if she isn't, then better she should be distanced from Noemi."

"Okay, I'll tell the Inspector. You can get back to your lunch now," he said, pointing to the sandwich, which Bella looked at with distaste, her appetite having evaporated during their conversation.

"Maybe…." Then she remembered what Noemi had said when she'd been trying to distract her. "Avi thought she'd known a Gabriel, though."

Carl was interested. "He did? She did?"

"Noemi told me. When she asked Nurit about Gabriel, Avi said he thought that was the name of someone she knew in London, someone she'd been seeing, someone from Africa."

"What did Nurit say?"

"That he was wrong, that that wasn't his name."

"It may be nothing, but I'll tell Inspector Martin. Thanks again. And be careful!"

∞

WHEN SHE GOT BACK to the store, Raoul told her about the policeman who'd been looking for her and wanted to know if he'd found her. She realized Raoul had never met Carl and considered teasing him, pretending the police were interested in her. But her usual flippancy deserted her as she considered her brother's request and she told him straightforwardly that the cop was her brother. She couldn't resist levity totally, though, and added, "Your other boss!"

Her brother's request preoccupied her for the rest of the afternoon. She didn't like the sound of danger, but she also didn't like the thought of Nurit putting her friends at risk. Was it possible she wasn't just spacey and weird, that she was also involved in something criminal? Bella didn't know her very well at all, had only met her a couple of times. But what about Mathieu? He'd known her much better. Wouldn't he have been able to tell? She remembered the time she'd seen them together, when Yolly was visiting. She'd been unfriendly, but Bella'd assumed that was because she wanted to keep him for herself.

And Mathieu! What about him? She was very fond of her neighbour.

If she was going to do what Carl had asked, she needed to know where Nurit was. She called Noemi at the hospital, who answered the phone herself. "Yes, I'm still in the hospital. But just until tomorrow, thank God. They only kept us this long because of some test they wanted to run."

"Is anything wrong?"

"No, no, at least I hope not. Nothing except the circumcision question of course."

Bella had completely forgotten about that. "You still haven't decided?"

"I've decided! I decided long ago! It's Avi who still hasn't decided to behave like a sane human being! He's out planning the ceremony now!" The new mother sounded decidedly less happy than when she'd answered the phone.

"With the cutting?" Bella ventured.

"Yes, with the cutting! He's talking to the *mohel*"

"The what?"

"The guy who does the snipping! Avi and his father went to talk to him."

That reminded Bella of her reason for calling in the first place. "Is Nurit with them?"

"No, she and her mother are getting the apartment ready for the baby."

Bella saw her opening. "Do they need help?"

"Maybe. The baby's room is sort of ready but it's got all this other stuff in there. They're moving it out."

"Is there room for everything? Won't it be too crowded?"

"We figured it out before, and there's room for everything. It'll be a bit crowded while they're all here, but after they leave there'll be room."

"Maybe Nurit can stay with Mathieu?" Bella would have more access to Nurit if she was staying downstairs.

There was a pause, then Noemi said hesitantly, "She was with someone else while she was away."

"Oh!" Bella didn't know what else to say.

"Poor Mathieu," said Noemi.

"Yes," Bella agreed.

"Do you think he liked her a lot?"

"I hope not."

"Me too!"

Bella shifted away from this uncomfortable topic. "So do you think I should go help them with the apartment?"

"That would be very nice of you," Noemi said. "My mother-in-law isn't up to much physical work – you saw how frail she is. Should I let them know you're coming?"

"No, I'll do that."

Bella got off the phone considering how best to attack her mission. Since her goal was to throw Nurit off balance, she should do everything she could to unnerve her. Surprise was probably helpful. Nurit had looked startled enough when she'd seen her the previous day. Remembering that Zelda and Mathieu had offered to help, she reflected that it might be even more unsettling if she showed up with one or both of them: Zelda was connected with the store and yarmulka, and Mathieu had a relationship with her, although she certainly didn't want him to get upset.

She didn't know what to do about Mathieu, so she started with Zelda, who enthusiastically agreed to meet her that evening. "Yes, and I can bring some oils and herbs to purify...."

Bella interrupted: "Maybe it's best not to bring anything just yet. I think it's kind of crowded right now, we're supposed to make order and room there."

Zelda sounded offended. "Oils and herbs do not take up room, they just make the space more welcoming and inviting."

Bella had been too intent on her plan to think about what Zelda might feel! She tried to cover up her tactlessness by backpedaling: "Yes of course, sorry, I was just trying to be efficient, I'm not used to baby stuff!"

Zelda was appeased and they agreed to meet when Bella closed the store.

Phew. That was the easy one. Maybe I shouldn't call Mathieu! She almost didn't. But the prospect of the helpless baby and mother at the mercy of a drugged-out addict propelled her forward. She decided to see how he felt before making up her mind.

"Hi Mathieu."

"Bella! What's up? Have you seen Noemi? Is she home?" He sounded like his old self.

"That's why I'm calling. She's coming home tomorrow and I'm going over there to make some room for the baby."

"Oh sure, I'll come help! That's why you were calling, isn't it?"

"Yes, but, first I need to tell you something.…"

"Okay…?"

No point beating about the bush. "Nurit's there."

"Oh!"

"Yes." When he said nothing more, Bella continued, "I wasn't sure how you'd feel about that."

"Hmmmm. Have you seen her? Nurit?"

"I did, just for a moment."

"I'm guessing she didn't mention me?"

"No…." Another silence. "So I totally understand if you don't want to come. I shouldn't even have asked."

"No, you know what? I'm glad you did. And I will come. It will be good to see her one last time, to make her tell me to my face it's over."

"Are you sure?" Bella was regretting her decision, this didn't seem like a good idea at all. She was letting her 'mission' get in the way of her friendships. But she couldn't get out of it now without telling Mathieu why, and that would be worse. Besides, she'd promised Carl she wouldn't. So she repeated her question, hoping Mathieu would bow out himself when he realized what it entailed. "Are you sure?"

"Yes! I'll show her I'm not upset!" was the immediate reply.

Bella felt even worse when she got off the phone, she shouldn't have done that. But she was stuck with it now. She would just have to unnerve Nurit without doing the same to Mathieu.

∞

EVEN THOUGH SHE still had Noemi's key, Bella rang the doorbell, so as not to startle Avi's mother. "Who is it?" she heard through the intercom.

When she responded, "Bella," the lock opened and the three of them climbed up to the third floor. Avi's mother greeted Bella like an old friend, despite having met her only once before; the fact that Bella could speak French had immediately endeared her to Avi's parents, whose English was minimal. Bella introduced her friends, saying they'd all come to help.

"Nurit," Mme Azoulay called towards the back of the apartment, "we have help. Thank you so much for coming – we are putting up all the Lilith amulets."

"The what?"

"Amulets to protect the baby from Lilith, until his circumcision. Lilith, the demon, who kills unprotected babies. The amulets will keep him safe for the first eight days." Bella saw Zelda's eyes light up with interest, but before the Wiccan could say anything, they heard Nurit's voice from the other room.

"Maybe now we can get this finished tonight!"

"Avi's not here?" Bella made conversation as they made their way towards the baby's room.

"No, he's out arranging with the *mohel*."

Bella stopped in time to keep her foot out of her mouth. *Do not discuss the circumcision,* she reminded herself, *under no circumstances discuss that. Let Noemi do it.*

Nurit had come out of the baby's room and was waiting when they got to the living room.

"Look at these nice friends of Avi's," her mother said, "they've come to help."

Nurit looked dumbstruck; her mouth opened but no sound came out.

"Nurit?" said her mother. "Is something wrong?"

"No, nothing," Nurit managed to stammer. "How nice of them, yes."

"We know Nurit," said Mathieu, who had prepared himself for this meeting.

"Yes, of course," said Nurit, "yes of course. How are you?" Primarily to Mathieu, although she included Zelda and Bella in her gesture.

"Fine," replied Mathieu. "We're just fine."

∞

SHE'D FORGOTTEN about Mathieu! She'd been so caught up in her problem that she'd totally forgotten him. She couldn't even remember exactly how they'd left things. Had she promised something that she hadn't done? Was she supposed to have been somewhere or done something? Was he mad at her?

Uh oh.... She didn't have a good feeling about this.

And she couldn't just go up and kiss him, or could she? What would her mother think, after the story about her supposed-lover in Toronto? Maybe her mother would just think she was a slut? She could live with that... what would Mathieu think though? Maybe he could even help her... she hadn't considered him when she was figuring out her options. But how likely was it that he had enough money to help her? He was just a librarian. He didn't even own his own apartment. Still, maybe she could stay with him until she figured out what to do, it was better than staying in an over-crowded apartment with her parents and a soon-to-be-arriving newborn probably-screaming baby.

It took her less than half a minute to think all this through, after which she threw herself at Mathieu, flung her arms around him, and planted a kiss on his lips. "I've missed you!" she exclaimed, trying to ignore the glares from both Bella and her mother.

Mathieu disentangled himself from her embrace and stepped back. "Where were you?" he asked.

The three others were also staring, waiting for her response. She faltered, then rallied, "I … I had to go away… for a day…"

"Why didn't you phone?"

"I…I'm so sorry." She tried to launch her breezy idiot act but his expression didn't change.

"Nurit?" her mother's voice cut into her frantic deliberations. "What's going on?"

Nurit couldn't come up with any answer that wouldn't land her in even more trouble, so she just stood there.

Zelda was the first to break the tableau. "We came to help," she said briskly to Avi's mother. "What can we do?"

With an anxious look at her daughter, she said "Yes, in here," and led the three helpers into the baby's room.

Nurit stayed glued to the floor in the living room, trying frantically to think what to do. Her impulse was to run, it didn't even matter where, just get out of here. NOW! But where could she go? What were her options?

Fact: There are at least two sets of people I have to watch out for. Both are dangerous: one for jail and the other for death or serious harm.

Option 1: disappear.

Pro: it would keep me out of jail and save my life.

Con: I don't know if it's possible. They're both very good at tracking people and both would be seriously pissed at me.

Also, I'm broke, it would take money to disappear and I just spent almost all I had on the trip to London. I don't have any money coming in because the stupid courier I hired to replace Gabriel got himself arrested. And in fact now they want even more money from me: they were already holding me responsible for Gabriel's loss. And now they're saying I owe them for Okonkwo's death as well.

So, even if I could disappear, it would be to live a homeless, faceless, friendless, familyless, moneyless existence, probably for the rest of my life. It would destroy my parents, I could never explain it to them. Even If I reached them, they wouldn't understand.

Where was I? She brought herself sternly back to the task at hand. *I think I got stuck on the negatives. Where are the positives?*

Oh no, that's not what I was doing; I was listing my options. So that was option 1, to disappear, not very appealing.

What's another choice?

Go on as before. Find another courier, make lots of money, pay them off. She liked this one, and brightened up until she remembered the cops dogging her. *Yes, that's a problem. A big problem. Unsurmountable? Maybe...* If the cops kept watching her, how could she conduct any business? Even if she could find a way, they would certainly notice the police shadow and, just as surely, not like it. Which meant they wouldn't be willing to do business with her. So she'd need to lose the tail. But how?

Even if she made it back to London, that wouldn't solve the problem – this Inspector whatever-his-name-was seemed to have been in touch with the police there, who might continue to keep an eye on her. She didn't think any of them had an inkling about the diamonds, but they weren't interested in diamonds, they were after her for murder. She started to shake. Those asinine thugs, what made them have an idiotic fight and get killed!

Maybe she could move somewhere else and continue her business from a different country? She perked up again at the possibility – *that's an idea worth pursuing. Of course, it depends on how persistent these cops are. But it's unlikely they'd care so much about me – who am I anyway?*

But she answered her own question immediately: *maybe they don't care about you personally, but they do care about your associates. They probably think you can lead them to the gang. No matter where you are. They would probably get Interpol interested in you...*

So I just have to stay away from Interpol's prying eyes! Unfortunately, she realized that those would be the same places where they would pay a lot more attention to her couriers, which would destroy her business anyway!

She was aware of the minutes ticking away as she stood there trying to figure out her future. So far, she'd failed to come up with any feasible plan.

Possibility 3 (or was she up to 4? - she couldn't remember): throw herself on her parents' mercy, confess everything to them and have them give her enough money to disappear. She rejected this option almost immediately. Even if she could bring herself to face the inevitable anguish this would cause, they didn't have enough money. Even if Avi chipped in, it wouldn't be enough. And they weren't good liars, so either the police or the gang (or both) would have no trouble getting the truth out of them.

She didn't know anyone who DID have enough money.

She was running out of options along with time.

She could always give herself up. Hideous as this prospect was, she might have to if there was no alternative. Maybe she could make a deal in exchange for her info, maybe even a good enough deal that there'd be no jail time, although that was unlikely. In any case, if she did do that, she would need hiding, maybe a changed identity. Would they do it for her? Even so, she'd be in serious danger. For the rest of her life. On the plus side, the Nigerians had very few, if any, officials on their payroll in North America. Yet. So, if she was going to do this, Montreal was a better choice than Israel or Europe.

When the doorbell rang, she jumped. *Who else can be coming? Can it get any worse?*

Her mother called out to her, and she replied, "Yes I'll get it," but she didn't move. It rang again, and her mother called to her again. "Okay, Okay, I'm going."

She made it to the intercom before it rang a third time. "Who is it?" she asked.

"Inspector Martin."

Oh no! What was he doing here? She hadn't figured out what to do yet; she needed more time. "What do you want now?" she screamed at the phone.

"To ask you a question."

"What question?"

She was still screaming, and her mother had appeared at her side, looking more concerned than ever. Luckily, the others were still in the baby's room.

"Can I come up?"

"No!" she screamed, at which her mother wanted to know what was happening. "Who is that, Nurit?"

She didn't want to tell her it was the police, she didn't want her mother to know anything about the police interest. Could she just hang up on him? Would he go away?

She tried that. "Someone who's been bugging me and won't leave me alone," she said to her mother.

Her mother said, "Give it to me, I'll get rid of him for you!" Before Nurit could get the phone back, her mother was saying, "Who is this?" firmly, then listening to the answer.

"Nurit, it's a policeman," she said. "he wants to ask you a few questions."

"Yes, I know, he's the one who won't leave me alone!"

"The police? But why?"

It was probably too late to run… she had a feeling she might have just run out of time.

Her mother buzzed in the inspector.

∞

THE INSPECTOR FOLLOWED Nurit and her mother into the living room. Bella, curious about the commotion, came out of the baby's room, but stopped when she saw the strange tableau. Zelda and Mathieu had followed her into the living room and stopped with her. They all stood motionless for a moment, then the inspector took charge.

"Hello," he said, looking at each of them in turn. "I've met some of you already." He nodded to Bella and Zelda. Turning to the others, he said: "I'm Inspector Stéphane Martin. I'm investigating the break-in at this woman's store," he indicated Zelda, "and the related murder of Toben Okonkwo, a Nigerian gangster."

Nurit's mother gasped: "Murder?" She collapsed on the sofa.

He nodded slowly, "Yes, murder."

"Who is this murdered person?" asked the old woman. "Does Nurit know him?"

"I don't know, that's what I'm here to find out."

Nurit found her voice: "No, I do not know him. As I've already told you."

Her mother looked puzzled: "Why do they think you know him?"

Nurit looked furious: "I DO NOT KNOW!"

Mme Azoulay looked at the inspector and asked the same question.

"We don't know if she knows him, we're just asking questions," he said mildly. "We just think it's possible that she knows him."

"I don't!" shouted Nurit.

"Why did you go to London this week?" he asked.

There was a moment of total silence. Then her mother looked at her: "London?"

Nurit was caught in her lie and couldn't see how to break free. Her world was unraveling, faster and faster. She'd told different lies to different people and they were here, in this room, together.

To make matters worse, Avi and her father came in just then and stood in the doorway, staring at the assembled

crowd. Nurit felt surrounded, trapped. None of her options were any good – she couldn't figure out what to
do…. What would happen if she stopped trying to figure
anything out and just made a run for it? So tempting …
just stop thinking and run … so very tempting…. Could
she dodge the people in the way, run down the stairs, and
keep going? Before she'd finished formulating the scenario, before she could stop herself, she realized she was
actually moving. She'd brushed her father and brother out
of the way and was already through the door and running
down the outside stairs.

The bottom of the stairs was blocked by a uniformed
policeman, standing next to the woman she'd seen at the
hospital along with the man she'd last seen at the airport
with Inspector Martin on her arrival from London.

∞

"I DON'T UNDERSTAND," whispered the old woman faintly,
as the Inspector left, presumably to follow her daughter. "I
don't understand." She looked at her son, but Avi shook
his head. The three neighbours, who had stood by and
watched the drama unfold, came to life and, without need-
ing to confer with each other, concluded it was best to
leave the family alone.

They murmured their good-byes, which were ignored
by the stunned Azoulays, and took their leave. By the time
they got downstairs, the street was empty – no Nurit and
no police.

"What just happened?" Zelda asked, more to herself
than because she thought she'd get an answer. But Bella,
feeling guilty about her part in the evening's activities, felt
obliged to answer. "The police think she's connected to
the break-in and death." The other two stared at her. She
went on, uncomfortable in the face of their shock. "Not

that she killed anyone. But that she knew something about who did."

Zelda was the first to speak. "How do you know that?"

"My brother told me. He's a cop." She decided not to mention the role she'd played – she wasn't feeling very good about having in any way contributed to the pain she'd witnessed. *But I did it to save Noemi and the baby, it's a good thing I did, to save that helpless baby.*

"So has she escaped now?" This was from Mathieu, who had finally found his voice.

"I don't think so – that inspector went after her pretty quickly."

"You think they arrested her?"

"I don't know." She didn't want to gain a reputation for being a police informant.

The three of them walked home in silence, all shocked by what they'd seen. They said quiet goodbyes and each went to their separate home.

Even Bella hadn't expected this. Her imagination had run to drug dealings, not links to murdered Nigerians.

Mathieu didn't know if he was relieved or devastated: Nurit's craziness had had nothing to do with him, but it also implied she'd been using him and hadn't really cared about him.

Zelda was initially the most stunned of the three, as she'd had no prior indication of Nurit's shenanigans. But, when she'd had a little time to think about it, she began to have an inkling of how the pieces might fit together: Daniel, Nurit, dangerous Africans, although she couldn't for the life of her see how her yarmulka entered into the picture. The fact that the police were onto Nurit made her a little more hopeful for Daniel's safety.

∞

WHEN HE'D GOTTEN the call saying that Bella had entered Nurit's house together with Zelda and Mathieu, Inspector Martin had had a good feeling. "This could be it!" he exulted to his partner as they drove over. He also phoned Carl to meet him there, to make sure she didn't get away if she tried to run for it. "All those people, together, plus her parents, this could be her breaking point."

And, sure enough, it had been. She'd run, literally, into the arms of his colleagues at the bottom of the stairs. When he'd followed and asked if she was ready to make a statement now, she'd nodded her head in resignation. When they got to the station, the first thing she said was: "I need protection!" She followed this with, "They'll kill me otherwise. I'm not saying a word unless you guarantee me protection."

It took a while. His captain took the request upstairs and a number of consultations took place at a higher level among various government agencies. The incursion into Canada of the notorious but hitherto-undetected Nigerian-based criminal organization NNM was discussed and counter-discussed. The desirability of obtaining as much information as possible about the group was affirmed by all the agencies who, eventually, came to the conclusion that it was worth the price of protection for the one potential informer. The nature of this protection was not specified, but the guarantee was given. Inspector Martin returned to the interview room where Nurit had sat, accompanied by coffee, cigarettes, and guard, during the time these negotiations took.

"Protection you will have," he said as he sat down opposite her.

"What kind?" She'd had time to think about all the ways she could be harmed for what she was about to do.

"We haven't worked that out yet but you have our word."

"What's that worth when I'm lying in a grave!" Her belligerent tone was a reflex left over from the persona she'd been until recently, she knew she had little choice. She'd already reviewed all her options and come up with a giant zero. Which was why she was here. So she had to trust them to protect her adequately. "Okay then," she said, reluctantly, "I guess we can go ahead."

"Good!" Martin jumped up, nodded to the guard, left the room, and returned a few minutes later with his partner and a tape recorder.

"Just one question before we start. This gives me immunity for my crimes, right?"

"If your information about the New Nigerian Movement is good, yes. I take it we're not talking murder?"

She shook her head. "No, definitely not murder."

"Okay then. What crime *are* we talking about?"

"Diamond smuggling."

He was completely taken by surprise – he'd been expecting her to say drug dealing. "Diamond smuggling?" he repeated. Realizing he hadn't turned on the recorder, he held up a hand, flipped the switch and introduced himself, the date and time, and participants. After doing this, he turned back to Nurit and said, "You were involved in diamond smuggling?"

"Yes. For the NNM. They got the diamonds to me and I got them to Israel."

Although this part was out of his jurisdiction, Martin was curious enough to ask: "How did you get into that?"

"It started before I left Israel. I met a man who dealt in diamonds. It's big business in Tel Aviv. He asked me if I wanted to make money, lots of money."

Martin let her talk, figuring he would stop or ask questions if he needed to. This wasn't part of his own investigation, but would probably be of interest to his superiors, especially if they ended up sharing with Interpol and/or assorted national police agencies. So he just nodded at her to continue.

She took a gulp of water and held up the empty bottle. Martin nodded at his partner, who left the room and returned a moment later with a new bottle. He gave it to Nurit, who took another swig, then put the bottle down. "Where was I?" she asked.

"About to make lots of money."

"Oh yes. Well, I was interested. He said all I had to do was go to England on a study visa and come back periodically with the diamonds, which a courier would bring to me. A percentage of the profits would be mine."

Martin nodded and Nurit continued.

"Of course, it wasn't quite that easy. But that was the basic idea. I had to contact the courier myself and work out the details, but they gave me his name. That was Gabriel."

"Ah! Gabriel…." They were getting to his investigation now.

"Gabriel was in England studying too. They had some hold on him, I don't know what, but they forced him to work with me."

"Was Gabriel Nigerian?"

"No, at least I don't think so, he didn't speak English all that well at first. He was from somewhere else in Africa. He brought the diamonds from Angola, maybe that's where he was from."

Martin signaled for her to go on.

"We would meet in class. Every four months. He would bring me a small bag with a couple of very high-quality diamonds, which I would then take to Israel and give to my friend."

"And you did this for how long?"

"Three years. Until Gabriel went missing."

"Just like that?"

She nodded. "And, unfortunately, for me at least, with a bag of diamonds."

"What happened then?" Somehow this story would make its way to Montreal...

"The NNM was pissed! And blamed me! Said it was my network, so my problem!" Two years later, she was still indignant about this patently unfair treatment.

"So they did what?"

"Made me pay for the diamonds AND the loss of Gabriel! I'm still paying it off. In the meantime, they found me another courier to bring the diamonds from Africa, but he was useless, got himself caught the first time he went through customs. And then it took a while, but they finally came up with someone halfway competent."

"And this was when?"

"About a year ago."

"So this past year you've been back to smuggling the diamonds and paying off your debt."

She nodded her agreement.

"So what happened? Here in Montreal?"

"I saw him!"

"Him?"

"Gabriel! I saw him! Just for a second, but I'm sure it was him! He had a distinctive look about him, and a distinctive walk. I saw him coming out of that store."

"*Objets*? The one that got broken into?"

"And then I saw those sparkly things in the window and I thought they were maybe the diamonds!"

He nodded encouragingly, so she continued: "So I called my NNM contact and told him about it. If I could give them back Gabriel and the diamonds, my debt would be canceled. And maybe I could even get back some of the money I've been paying them for the last two years."

"This contact was in Canada?"

"I don't know where he was, I've never met him. But he said there were a couple of guys in Canada, scoping things out. He gave me a number for them and told me to get a new burner phone for it. And this guy in Canada would give me a new number for him as well, as this one might be compromised."

"So you got the phone and called?"

"To set it up. We met at that warehouse and I explained it to them. I couldn't go near the store in case I ran into someone I knew, but I told them where it was and about Gabriel and the diamonds. They were just supposed to watch the store, wait for Gabriel to show up, grab him, grab the diamonds, and split. It should have been simple, easy, clean."

Except for poor Gabriel. Martin left this thought unvoiced so she wouldn't think he was judging her. He settled for: "But it wasn't?"

"No…. They took turns watching the store. One of them, this Okonkwo guy, got impatient, I don't know where they even found him! It's like he'd never done this before! So he got impatient and figured Gabriel wasn't going to show up because it had been two days since I'd seen him. So Okonkwo decided to just go ahead on his own, grab the diamonds and get out of there."

"So he broke the window…?"

Nurit nodded. "… and grabbed the wool thing. Which had sparkly things on it. Which were not diamonds, as it turned out."

"And where were you during these events? Did you witness them yourself?"

"No, I wasn't there, I was hiding out waiting for their call to tell me it was done. But the call never came and when I finally went to check, there were cops so I couldn't go near the warehouse. I couldn't find the guys, I couldn't find out anything. I only knew what I could get out of

Mathieu. I only found out this week what happened! When I managed to get hold of my contact, he told me. That they weren't diamonds. And that Gabriel never showed."

"How did Mr. Okonkwo end up dead?"

"I'm not sure – my contact didn't go into details. I think it was an accident. But the other guy left Montreal, maybe even Canada, I don't know where he went."

"And the Mayan statue?"

"The what?"

"The statue that was taken from the window? The valuable old Mayan figure?"

"I don't know anything about that."

"Just one more thing for me: have you been selling drugs?"

"No, of course not!"

Inspector Martin raised his eyebrows at her moral outrage, but restrained his tongue. He ended the interview and prepared to pass the informant on to the other agencies. "This is it for us, you'll be leaving now, talking to other agencies, then going into the system. Do you want to say good-bye to your family first? You won't be able to contact them again after this."

Nurit swallowed hard. She hadn't contemplated that aspect. And, much as she was afraid to face the hurt in her parents' eyes, she didn't think she could live with herself if she didn't at least say good bye to them. "Yes, I guess I'd better do that."

∞

SHE'D PROBABLY BEEN telling the truth but Inspector Martin had to check before he could close the file. Sébastien's mother let him in and followed him into the living room where her son was lying on the couch, eyes closed and headphones blaring so loud he could hear the music from outside the room. When she pulled them from Sébastien's ear to get his attention, her son opened his eyes sleepily, then sat up hastily when he saw the officer.

"Well?" demanded his mother. "Did you find the criminal who assaulted my son?"

"Yes, but he's dead." He told them the whole story.

"Wow," said the boy. "What a thing to get in the middle of!"

"Yes, you were definitely unlucky."

"You know, that piece of clay…"

"Yes?"

"I've been thinking about it … haven't had much else to do while lying here…. I think I remember reaching out to break my fall after he stabbed me. I was falling against the broken window, the broken glass. And when I put out my hand to break the fall, I think I may have grabbed something, like that statue. I don't remember too clearly, but I have a sort of vague memory of it."

"You don't know what happened to the rest of it? You only had a piece in your pocket."

"No, sorry, that's all I remember. Maybe I dropped it somewhere."

"Thanks, that's a big help. You were found a couple of blocks away, I'll look in the other streets. In any case, it's all over now, there's nothing to be afraid of. And I hope you're healing okay?"

"Yes, thank God!" His mother also looked relieved. "Not that we thought it was anything personal, but still… it's good to know it's finished." Her tone softened. "Inspector, would you like some coffee?"

"I'd love a glass of water, thank you."

When she left the room, he brought out a picture of Nurit and showed it to Sébastien. "Is this the woman you bought drugs from?"

He shook his head. "Nope, that's not her."

Seems like the Azoulay woman was telling the truth. "Have you talked to your parents yet?"

He shook his head again. "They haven't mentioned it … maybe they don't know?" he added hopefully. "You won't tell them?"

Martin nodded. "I'll stay out of it – it's nothing to do with me or my case, just between you and the hospital."

Sébastien's mother walked outside with him. "Is my son in trouble?"

Martin looked at her inquiringly.

"Because of the drugs?" she added.

The inspector shook his head. "I think he's afraid of you though."

"We haven't decided yet what to do, so we haven't mentioned it."

"Maybe that's a good plan, having him uncertain and afraid of you!"

∞

WHEN AVI BROUGHT his wife and son home, the apartment they entered felt more like a house of mourning than one celebrating a birth. His parents sat, side by side, silent and unmoving, on the couch. Exactly as he'd left them several hours before, when they'd returned from their goodbye visit with Nurit. Avi had offered his arm to help on the stairs, but both had refused, and each one had walked alone, slowly, up the outside stairs, and then, even more slowly, to the top floor. When they got inside, they made it to the living room, where they sat down on the couch, where they still were.

When they heard the baby's cries, the statues came to life. His mother smiled feebly and tried to stand up, but it was as if she'd forgotten how, her legs didn't know what to do. His father tried to help her, but he crumpled back against the sofa's cushions, where he lay, looking perplexed. His wife, who hadn't noticed his efforts, still tried to make sense of the act of standing.

Noemi was so shocked by the sight that she also stood motionless, her arms outstretched in a gesture of unrequited greeting. Avi had warned her that they were distraught but she hadn't expected to see them so diminished. Avi was the only one capable of movement in that moment. He brought the baby he was carrying into the room, deposited the baby-carrier on the floor, put his arm around his mother and helped her to her feet. Then he went over to his father and helped him back to an upright seated position. By this time, Noemi had regained movement and she also came over to the couch. She took her mother-in-law's hands into hers and held them for a moment, then wrapped the tiny-looking woman in her arms and held her tightly.

Again, it was the baby's cries that broke the tableau. Noemi let go of her mother-in-law, saying "I think he's hungry. Again." She tried for a note of levity by adding, "Just like a man!" Her mother-in-law smiled, as weakly as before, either at Noemi's joke or just the sound of her voice

Week 8

*He started preparing for his departure. He had never been out of the
country, had only left his city during occasional school field trips. A
small suitcase held his few belongings. The only thing he hesitated over
was the amulet his mother had given him; the intricately carved native
bird had stayed with him from the moment she'd given it to him. It
was all he had left of his parents and it had never left his side, protecting both Fernando and himself. But now he wondered which of
them needed it most. Both of them faced uncertainty and danger. In
the end, he took it to a jeweler and had him cut the tiny figure in two,
right down the middle. He gave one half to Nando and kept the other
for himself; now they could both benefit from their mother's protection,
no matter where they were or how far apart.*

*Saying goodbye was one of the hardest things he'd ever done,
maybe even harder than living through the violence and losing his parents. That last week, the neighbourhood children hardly left them
alone, taking an obvious pleasure in taunting him mercilessly about
'abandoning' his brother, about being better than the rest of them.
They had never forgiven him for his ambitions or success, and took
this last opportunity to make his life a misery.*

*Minutes before he had to leave, they managed to find a private
spot. They held onto each other, wordlessly, their tears mingling; then
he pressed the half amulet into Nando's hand. "She'll always be with
you now too," he whispered into his brother's hair before giving him
one last bone-squeezing embrace. "Stay safe," he said, and ran to
catch his ride.*

∞

NOEMI LEFT THE HOUSE QUIETLY, trying not to feel like she
was sneaking out. True, she hadn't told anyone where she
was going, but she didn't have to. She was a grown woman,
going out with her baby. Her own baby, who was completely swaddled inside his sling. They probably wouldn't
even notice she wasn't there. Her in-laws had barely moved

since returning from Nurit's leave-taking. And Avi hadn't been much better. She'd told him she was going out, but wasn't sure it had registered. All three of them sat there, hour after hour, silent and blank, as if they were mourning, sitting shiva. Nurit hadn't died, but they would probably never see her again. They hoped that this change, drastic as it was, would save her life, but could make no sense of it. Her parents couldn't even talk. Avi could and had gone on and on at great length: how could this have happened? how could Nurit, his little sister, have done those things, gotten involved with those criminals? He'd thought he knew her, seeing through her lies and deceptions, but never, nowhere, no way, had he come close to imagining a scenario like this! Noemi hadn't either, but she wasn't as surprised. She'd never felt a connection to her sister-in-law, although, like Avi, she'd suspected her more of self-centredness than smuggling and gangsters.

In any case, she was sure the mood in the house was bad for the baby; she knew it was bad for her. And it was not going to improve, at least not for her, in the immediate future; tomorrow was the circumcision, when they were going to cut, to snip, to mutilate her precious baby. And she was going to sit there and watch them do it.

In the end, she'd agreed. Avi's parents had been so completely devastated about their daughter. They'd looked so old, their sunken faces so skeletal. The only spark of life was when they looked at their grandson. She just didn't have the heart to take that away from them, to make that another incomprehensible problem for them to confront.

Avi had of course never even mentioned the possibility to them, so there was no need for any explanations.

But Noemi was seriously distressed about the mutilation her precious baby would endure. She was worried about what it would do to him, how it would affect his very being. She didn't really believe in Zelda's New Agey stuff, but how could it not affect him? At this so-vulnerable age, when he hadn't had time to develop any defenses. That was her job, she was his mother.

She'd been moaning to Zelda, the only person who seemed to share her concerns. She'd gone over there for anther disgusting-tasting herbal tea to help with the after-birth and had stayed for several hours, soothed by the calm atmosphere and the older woman's sympathy. Zelda had proposed a solution of sorts: her coven could perform a protection ritual before the circumcision, to surround the baby with a circle of magic energy. Noemi had no idea if she believed in any of this, but had accepted the offer any-way. It wasn't all that different from the amulets her mother-in-law put up for protection.

So here she was, sneaking out of her house to take her baby to a Wiccan ceremony that would protect him from the Jewish ritual he would undergo tomorrow. She hadn't mentioned it to Avi; he was so on edge, this might well have tipped him over. Her husband was not the calmest of men; she loved him, but preferred him in his calmer moods.

She tried to quell her anxiety as Zelda took the sleeping baby from her. When the newborn's eyes opened, Zelda rocked him gently until they closed again. Noemi watched carefully as he was placed in a basket sitting in the middle of the room, and allowed herself to be guided to the empty space awaiting her, completing the circle. She stayed watchful, alert for any sign of discomfort, but the infant slept on, through the lighting of the candles and incense, through the chants, even through the sprinkling of water. When he was placed back in her arms, he stirred slightly, and snuggled even closer to her; she thought she saw a small smile on the tiny mouth.

∞

BELLA WENT TO MEET Zelda at *objets*; they were going to the circumcision together. She knocked on the door; when nobody answered, she pushed lightly and realized the door was open. Worried that they might be late, she stepped inside, calling to Zelda. She glanced around the darkened room and stopped suddenly when she saw the small table in the centre. With the only light in the room focused on it. Or rather, on the object on top of it. She forgot to breathe; she could only stare. She couldn't look away, not even when she heard Zelda's voice beside her. "Do you like it?"

She found her voice, and stammered, "Is-is that for me?"

"I hope so," was the reply. "But only if you like it."

"Yes!" When she realized she'd shouted, she lowered her voice. "Yes!" she repeated at normal volume, "it's beautiful!"

When she still stood in the same spot, Zelda moved towards the table. "Do you want to try it on?"

"Oh yes!" she said, but without moving. She was completely mesmerized by the yarmulka sitting there waiting for her. She realized it was impossible, but she felt as if it were talking to her, calling to her, waiting for her. It was as if it had cast a spell on her.

Meanwhile, Zelda had picked up the yarmulka and brought it to her. It was much louder and more ornate than she'd anticipated: it was blue, as she'd requested, but even in the pale light, the feathers, buttons, and wool shimmered and glowed. Her inner voice was telling her she couldn't possibly wear anything like that, even as she bent forward so Zelda could place it on her head. She put her hands up and touched it reverently. It felt like it belonged there, like it had always been there, and like it would always be there. It felt somehow very right. She looked into the mirror that Zelda brought and saw that it even looked very right, somehow not quite as flamboyant as she'd feared, but also not quite as inconspicuous as her usual look. It looked, and with it on her head she found that she looked, beautiful. Clearing her throat several times before she could get a word out, she finally managed to wrench her eyes away to thank the artist.

When she did, she saw that Zelda was holding a yarmulka herself, one that looked very familiar. She forgot her own newly-created magnificence as she realized what it was. "Is that your yarmulka?" she asked excitedly. "Did you get it back?"

The smile that lit up Zelda's face was answer enough; she also seemed too overcome with emotion to speak. What was it about these objects that could affect them so strongly?

"It looks like new!"

"Yes," Zelda nodded. "It wasn't as badly torn as I'd thought; it was really only around the largest crystal, which had been ripped off. I fixed it up, but decided not to replace that stone; in any case, that one was irreplaceable, it belonged to my mother," her face fell as she contemplated the loss, then picked up again, "but I've brought her energy back into the yarmulka even without it, and certainly neither of us wants it stolen again!"

"It is gorgeous again and doesn't look battered at all. But I think I like mine better!"

"I'm so glad you like it," was the reply. "I was so happy to get mine back, the energy that got crocheted into yours was exhilerating! Do you feel it?"

"I do!" Bella replied. "I do feel that! But how can that be?"

"I cast a spell on it. Mainly of protection, but also gratitude. The protection will keep you safe. I recast the spell on mine at the same time, it needed to be purified first, then I gave it a double layer of protection."

Could it be that Zelda's spells really worked? Nonsense, of course, Bella knew that. Still, she couldn't deny the fact that something about the yarmulka felt very special, as if it had a personal bond with her.

As they turned to go, on their way to a Jewish ritual, wearing their Jewish yarmulkas protected by Wiccan blessings, Bella finally remembered to ask the question that had been in her mind ever since she'd met Zelda. "How can you be both Wiccan and Jewish?"

Zelda explained that Wicca was a very inclusive religion, that it had no problem with multiple gods, multiple rituals, that it didn't demand any kind of exclusive commitment, no proclamations of faith or dogmatic assertions. While she realized that Judaism might not have the same attitude, she didn't really care as she wasn't a practicing Jew. She'd been brought up with it, but hadn't done anything herself since leaving her parents' home. She'd never felt that it spoke to her. However, she did feel the heritage and the history of Judaism; it was "in her blood", whatever that meant.

As Bella was digesting this very different image of Judaism, she saw that Zelda was holding something else in her hands. "I made one for Yolly too. Do you think she'll like it?" She looked more closely and saw that it was a deer-stalker-yarmulka, a head covering that could do double duty: sacred rituals and detecting. "I think she'll love it! It's perfect for her."

It was Zelda who'd invited Yolly to the circumcision. She'd been grateful for the 11-year-old's persistence in uncovering the truth. After Inspector Martin had explained the what, why, and how to her, she knew that she and her store were not, and had never been, targets. It made her feel a whole lot safer about the location, about being in the store by herself. It even eased some of her anxiety about Daniel (or Gabriel, as she supposed she should call him).

She'd always felt that he lived in constant fear, that he kept looking over his shoulder. This was probably still true, but the chain of contacts was broken; hopefully the trail was now muddy enough that he could try to make a new life somewhere else. She said many prayers for him, and sent her blessings throughout the world, hoping they would find him and keep him safe.

So Zelda had called Yolly to thank her. It was not only because of her, the police might have gotten onto Nurit anyway, but Yolly's detectiving had helped point the way. Bella had told her about Yolly's dogged insistence that she was right and her unrelenting reminders to follow up. Zelda was a great believer in knowing the truth; she was sure that it was always better than to live with lies. It was not knowing that got in people's way; once they knew what was going on, they could make decisions and get on with their lives. She saw in Yolly a similar attitude, although she realized she might be projecting, especially as she'd never even met her. But she'd been touched by what Bella and Noemi had told her about the little detective's dedication to uncovering truth and had called to tell her so.

As it turned out, she'd been the one to tell Yolly what had happened. Still in the country with her family, Yolly had realized she couldn't do anything more from so far away. Bella was too unreliable to act as her 'agent'; it would just have to wait until she got back to the city and could act for herself. In the meantime, she'd given herself over to playing with her sisters, and was in the lake racing with Molly while Polly timed them when she called. Lila had sounded surprised when Zelda'd asked to speak with her oldest daughter, but said she'd give her the message.

When Yolly called her back several hours later, she didn't know at first who Zelda was. When she realized what it was about, Zelda could hear the excitement mounting in her voice. Before she could even thank her, when

Yolly realized she'd been vindicated and proved right, as opposed to the deceitful deceiving lying two-faced gangster-associated villain who'd tried to blacken her name, Yolly began shouting "YES!YES!YES!" non-stop. Zelda heard a clunk as the phone dropped to the floor and the excited shouts became fainter as if Yolly was getting further away. After a minute or two, Lila came on the phone and Zelda explained the situation to her. "I just wanted to thank her," she explained to an incredulous Lila. "Who knows if they would have caught them if not for her?"

When a quietened Yolly grabbed the phone back, Zelda managed to thank her, which sent Yolly off again, although she returned more quickly this time. Infected with some of the 11-year-old's enthusiasm, Zelda asked if she'd like to come to the circumcision with them. She wasn't sure what had prompted her; perhaps the sense that she should do something concrete to acknowledge her gratitude. And she had a feeling that Yolly would appreciate the invitation, the public recognition of her success. It was only afterwards that Zelda was hit with the thought that the Azoulays might not be so happy to see the person who had precipitated their family disaster, but she hoped they would either not realize the part Yolly had played, or not hold it against her.

Yolly was delighted to be invited to a 'grownup' ceremony. With her new grownup friends, including the 'cool' Moroccan woman. And without her parents. She shouted "yes" without even consulting Lila, who was still hovering around uncertainly. She handed the phone to her mother when Zelda suggested it, then trained unblinking eyes on Lila until she heard her say the magic words. "Yes, I guess that's ok. I can put her on the bus to town if you and Bella pick her up." At which point she ran through the small cottage and out into the yard, turning cartwheels before collapsing on the ground. "My first solved case!" she announced to the Sherlock Holmes of her imagination. "The Yarmulka in the Window!"

For Yolly, Zelda had created a fuchsia deerstalker-yarmulka, reminiscent of the hat Sherlock Holmes had made famous but with a few added feathers and crystals, as thanks and gratitude for the part the young detective had played in solving the 'case' and for, hopefully, helping keep Daniel safe, wherever he was. Yolly was so touched by the present she was rendered speechless, then launched herself at Zelda and clutched her as tightly as she could, only letting go to firmly pull the hat onto her head as if she would never take it off.

∞

By the time they left for the *brit milah*, the circumcision, Noemi almost felt ready. Resigned at least. A part of her was still hoping to somehow find a way out, but most of her realized that wasn't going to happen. Despite her convictions, despite her firm beliefs, she was going to present her child as an offering for a barbaric ceremony. "You saved Abraham's son at the last minute," she screamed silently to the god she didn't believe in, "why not mine?" She wasn't surprised when the non-existent god made no reply.

The offering was to take place in a big fancy synagogue. Avi had found a Sephardic one not far from their neighbourhood; although Montreal had many synagogues, the majority were Ashkenazi, following Eastern European traditions. Avi himself didn't care, he'd never set foot in a synagogue in all the time they'd been living here. But it mattered to his father, who was a regular participant in a Moroccan congregation in Israel. He and his father had met with the cantor, who was a licensed and experienced *mohel*. The fact that he was also Moroccan had been especially pleasing to his father.

Noemi had never been in the synagogue before, and when she realized it required segregation between men and women, she almost turned around and left. But the sight of Avi's mother stopped her. Not only did the elderly woman look more alive, she was walking like a person rather than a zombie. Noemi could only too easily imagine the look of incomprehension that would result if she walked out now - it would be the same one she'd been seeing all week, if not worse. Noemi would be plunging another dagger into her already broken heart; she didn't think her own heart could survive that. So she swallowed her outrage and followed the others into the chapel, where the *mohel* awaited his victim.

As soon as she got inside, a woman came towards her with arms outstretched to receive the baby. As she hesitated, she realized the room was filled with strangers, mostly men. Who were all these people? She became aware of the background sounds, realized that she was hearing 'Moroccan' for the first time since arriving in Montreal. She'd grown up with this Arabic dialect, it was what her family and neighbours had spoken. Although not religious, they'd held onto their cultural identity; the language and the food had formed the background to her 'Israeli' life. Hearing it now gave her a strange sense of belonging which was at odds with the extreme malaise she was feeling in the religious setting where her baby was about to be mutilated. The woman still waited, her smile starting to fade. Noemi made herself move. She looked for a last time on her 'whole' baby boy, and gave her precious son over, knowing that when she got him back, he would have been changed irrevocably: lost a foreskin and gained a name. She hoped Zelda's magic was strong enough. She went to sit next to her mother-in-law at the front of the women's section. From the row behind, Zelda gave her shoulder an encouraging squeeze: "It'll be okay; you don't have to worry."

Bella, sitting next to Zelda, gave her an inquiring look. Zelda whispered: "Baby protection," as if that explained anything. *More magic!* Bella marveled at how much of Zelda's 'witchcraft' had been picked up by Noemi, but kept quiet. Yolly, on her other side, had already pricked up her ears and she didn't want to take the chance of her erupting in her usual fashion. For the moment, she was being un-characteristically still. Bella smiled to herself at the image: the three of them in this traditional synagogue adorned in their distinctly unconventional yarmulkas! On Yolly's other side, Sophie looked strangely bare-headed by com-parison as she waved discretely to Michael, sitting by him-self among the elderly congregants in the men's section. He'd not yet had his Bar Mitzvah, so technically he could have sat with the women, but as he was already taking the preparatory lessons, he'd preferred this. Sophie wished Mathieu had come to keep Michael company, but he was still heartbroken over Nurit, and didn't think the sight of a baby being cut would cheer him up. Yolly also waved to Michael, a little more enthusiastically than his mother. So-phie was glad to see a small smile appear at the corner of her son's mouth as he gave an answering, but much sub-tler, wave to the 11-year-old sitting next to her.

Bella turned forward; the ritual was beginning. The woman who had finally received the baby from the reluc-tant mother gave it over to one of the elderly men at the front. He, in turn, placed the infant on a large empty chair. The man who seemed to be in charge mumbled some words that Bella couldn't understand. She heard Sophie whisper "Elijah's chair," probably to Yolly; Bella wondered if her cousin understood that any better than she did. She caught a glimpse of the faces in front of her: Noemi was white and completely immobile, but her mother-in-law wore a serene smile.

Another man came forward and picked up the baby-bundle; he brought it over to Avi, who grew in stature as he swelled with pride. He looked so happy that, for a moment, Noemi was almost glad she'd chosen to do this. Then her fear and anxiety returned as Avi took the baby up to his own father, who was sitting in the other large chair ready to receive his grandson. The frail old man was also transformed: when the baby was placed in his lap, the man in his place was one Noemi had not seen since their wedding, when his delight had infused them all with hope for the future. Turning sideways, she saw the same smile on the face of a younger and very proud grandmother. In that moment, Noemi was actually glad she'd said yes and she tried to hold on to this feeling as a suddenly pale Avi picked up a deadly-looking scalpel and shakily handed it to the *mohel*. After a few call-and-response recitations, which Noemi prayed would go on forever, the moment of no-return arrived. She tried not to flinch or cry out as the officiant brought the scalpel to her baby's tiny penis. She was determined not to look away; as the one who had already failed in her duty to protect him against all harm, she owed it to him to share the pain as much as possible.

To Noemi's surprise, there was no scream. Only a quiet whimper betrayed the fact that the deed was done, a whimper immediately quelled as the wine-dipped swab was placed in the baby's mouth. She wished there was a similar sedative for her! Even Avi was holding on to the back of Elijah's Chair as if he might keel over.

Another elderly man came forward; he picked the baby up from his grandfather's lap and stood holding him, facing towards the *mohel*, who had abandoned his cutting implement and now held the glass of red wine that Noemi was coveting. He blessed the wine and then gave her son his name along with two drops of wine. After eight days of being Baby Azoulay, now that he'd joined the covenant by forfeiting his foreskin, he became Nahum Uri, bearing the same name as his grandfathers, one of whom stood proudly beside him. Avi, restored to his expanded stature, joined them and they stood still for a moment: three generations of Azoulay men.

"So strange," Sophie murmured. "To name the baby after a relative who's still alive."

"That's like me!" Bella shushed her cousin, whose 'whisper' had reverberated throughout the chapel. Yolly finished her explanation in Sophie's ear: "it's a Moroccan thing."

The man holding the baby drank from the wine, which was then brought over to Noemi, so she could share in the blessing. She restrained herself, decorously taking only a polite sip. She knew the ordeal was almost over and soon she would be able to drink more, much more. She could wait as they blessed the spices, recited a prayer for Nahum Uri's soul, and, finally, recited the prayer for his recovery, to which Noemi, along with the rest of the congregation, replied with a heartfelt "amen." And then her precious baby was returned to her.

Bella stayed behind with Zelda and Noemi as the rest of the participants made their way to the food waiting in the hall next door. Yolly had run ahead to join Michael, and Sophie followed them. After a few moments, Noemi realized she wasn't alone and raised her head. Through the tears streaming down her face, she said, "It's okay, you go eat, I'll just stay here for a few minutes."

"Is he okay?" Bella asked falteringly.

"Sound asleep - probably from all that wine!"

"Are you okay?" Zelda asked.

"No, but I will be. I'll just sit here for a little longer. You go," was the reply. "Thank you for the protection spell - it seems to have worked."

"So glad." Zelda said as she and Bella made their way into the food room. Bella held her tongue, keeping her skepticism to herself. Besides, she wasn't absolutely certain that it hadn't worked. Nahum Uri (she had to stop thinking of him as 'Baby Azoulay') didn't seem traumatized. Although, as Noemi had said, that could also be the wine.....

She and Zelda joined Sophie, who was watching Michael and Yolly heap their plates full of the kind of food that Bella recognized from dinners at Avi and Noemi's. The three of them followed the children's example with a little more self-control and stood self-consciously in a corner, nibbling on the Jewish Moroccan delicacies, waiting for their friend. Avi was too difficult to approach for the moment, standing with his parents in a circle of well-wishers. He did see them, though, and mouthed a "thank you" to Bella before he was reclaimed by his mother.

When Noemi made her appearance, she and Nahum Uri were immediately claimed by the well-wishers, who escorted them over to the rest of the family. A beaming Avi took Nahum Uri and placed him into the arms of his radiant mother; he kept his own arms in place for support as she gazed down blissfully at her now covenanted grandson. With her hands free, Noemi went to get herself the glass of wine she'd been craving since seeing the scalpel. She took a healthy swig; then, remembering that she was breast-feeding, reluctantly left the rest of the alcoholic beverage untouched.

When she rejoined her family, her friends made their way over as well. "Mazel tov!" This from Sophie, the first one to speak. "Isn't this amazing! Look at all these people who don't even know you, who came today just to be part of this celebration."

Noemi was still having trouble thinking of it as a celebration, but even she had to admit it was kind of wonderful to see all these strangers gathering just to wish them well.

She retrieved her precious baby from his grandmother, whose arms were beginning to sag, and they both gazed in admiration and pride at the youngest member of their family.

"If only Nurit could have been here," said her mother, becoming a frail old woman again, then, shaking her head, retransformed into the prouder younger version. "But today is for celebrating, not for mourning."

∞

WHEN BELLA GOT off the bus, it was already dark. She checked out the surrounding street more carefully than she would have a month ago, before the break-in and other suspicious goings on. As she made her way towards home, she heard a footstep and spun around to see Emkay emerge from a dark doorway. They stared at each other for a second, then Emkay grinned. "Bel, you old fart, what are you doing out so late? Isn't this past your bedtime?"

Bella was too tired for banter. "What are you doing here?"

"Just hanging…," was the casual reply.

Neither seemed able to come up with anything else to say, so they stood in silence until Emkay broke it. "Actually, I'm off, I probably won't see you again, at least not for a while."

"Oh! How'd you get the money to take off with?"

"Oh, you know … a little of this, a little of that …."

The image of the butt that Yolly'd found surfaced in Bella's mind. "You've been selling drugs!"

"Just a little weed."

Bella also remembered Mathieu's exchange with Emkay in the park. "To kids?"

Emkay shrugged. Bella stared in disbelief at this person she had once known. Emkay continued blithely: "Sure you won't change your mind and come with me?"

This reminded Bella of their past friendship, she almost smiled despite herself. "No, I don't think so. But thanks for the offer."

"Okay … your loss. Don't get too stuck in the mud, Bel."

Thank god she's leaving, so I don't have to be the one to stop her! I guess the drug problem had nothing to do with a notorious and violent gang moving into our neighbourhood – that's a relief, one less thing to worry about!

∞

WHEN INSPECTOR MARTIN got back from his day off, he found the report waiting on his desk. The expert archaeologist had finally returned from his dig and found their specimen waiting for him; it had taken him no time at all to ascertain that it was indeed Mayan, but certainly not ancient: he estimated its age as approximately five years old. If they needed him to, he could run some tests to try to pinpoint it more precisely. He would wait to hear back before proceeding.

So much for the valuable ancient statue. He decided to waste no more time looking for it and closed the file.

∞

Epilogue

My dearest Zelda

I apologize most profusely for all the trouble I have caused you. You have been a very good friend to me, so kind and generous, and I am so very sorry to have caused all these problems in return. I wish I could come and see you and say these things to your face, but it is not safe, and I do not want to involve you in any more danger, so I must make do with this weak substitute of words on paper.

First, I must tell you, my name is not Daniel. It is Gabriel. I was born in Angola, during a long and violent war. My parents were killed, and my little brother and I went to live with our neighbours.

When the war was finally over, I thought my brother and I could have a good life. I worked hard at school and was given a scholarship to study at the London School of Economics.

But just before I left for England, my neighbour's uncle came to see me. He'd always been with UNITA, who continued to fight against the government even after they lost the war. This uncle told me that I must help him or he would take away my little brother and make him a soldier. I must not tell anyone, not even his niece, or he would kill Fernando.

I did not know what to do. I didn't want to help them, but I was so frightened for my brother. I knew how dangerous these people were, I had seen the results my whole life. I could see no alternative, so I agreed. He said I must take diamonds with me from Angola to England. Not very many each time: most of the smuggled diamonds crossed the border easily into Nigeria and then to India, where they were mixed with legal ones. But they were concerned that the finest diamonds would be 'lost' along the way, so they had a different plan for the high-end gems, which would land them in Israel instead. And they'd figured out a route that fit in perfectly with my own plans. Each time I went from Angola to England, every four months, I was to take a small bag containing a few stones. Their Israeli contact in England would give me the instructions for passing them on.

I was to tell absolutely no one about any of this, I was to follow the instructions exactly, and my brother and I would both live to a fine old age.

I did this for two years, going back and forth with the diamonds. But from the beginning, I was thinking of how to get out of this. I watched and waited and planned. I found a way to get my brother out, but it was very expensive, so I took one of their bags of diamonds to pay for it. I got him to a safe place, far away, and then I too disappeared. I came to Montreal and changed my name. I knew they would look for us, but I hoped we were far enough that they would not find us. There are not many Angolans in Canada so I thought I'd be safe. I met you, and the rest you know.

I was starting to breathe more easily (thanks as well to your excellent training in meditation and chanting) and enjoy our life here. When I saw the beautiful objects you were creating, I even allowed myself to make the bird masks as my father had taught me. But then, last month, I saw my English contact. Here. In Montreal. On the same street as our store. I could not believe it. How could life be so cruel? I saw her only out of the corner of my eye, but it was enough. Just to be absolutely certain, before I had to turn my back on this life I had come to love, I hid and watched as she approached the store. It was definitely her. And I was fairly certain she'd seen me.

I knew I had very little time before she sent them after me, so I left immediately. I passed through Winnipeg on my way to get Fernando, and took the chance of sending you a message through your sister's grandson. Now we are far away.

I wish I could see you again, but it is not possible. Thank you for everything you did. I am more grateful than any words can express. I will always remember you.

Daniel / Gabriel

∞

BELLA GAVE THE letter back to Zelda. "Thank you for showing me this."

"My coven met again. We sent the protection throughout the world so, wherever he is, he'll be safe."

"I really hope so. I'd even be prepared to believe in your magic if it could make that true," Bella replied.

Sonia Zylberberg is the author of *Too Many Latkes* and *The Orange on the Seder Plate*, the first two books in the Bella mystery series. She lives in Montreal, where she teaches at Dawson College and reads mystery novels in her spare time. You can find her on Facebook or visit her website: www. soniaz.weebly.com.